Black Vigilantes
Thah Xah Qshunah

Tracy L. Davis and Kenya S. Moore

Cadmus Publishing
www.cadmuspublishing.com

Published by Cadmus Publishing
www.cadmuspublishing.com
Port Angeles, WA

ISBN: 978-1-63751-366-8

Dedication:

This book is dedicated to the struggle against oppression and those who strive for true and meaningful social justice reform.

It's dedicated to all the people who marched in the streets, and all those who continue to march today.

Keep pushing y'all.

Change gone come.

Acknowledgements

During this time that I've been incarcerated, I've learned a lot. I've dealt with thousands of people in one form or another on a daily basis for nearly three decades. But none have stood out to me more than Bloods, Folks, and Crips and the Spanish gangs. These guys practically raised me in prison. Teaching me what it means to be loyal, respectful, and to have the courage of a lion; not to mention the importance of family and brotherly love. As I looked at these groups of men more closely, it became clear that these were the men that could bring real change to all of our Black and Brown communities if only they could find the means and will to unite themselves and focus their energy towards the collective upliftment of our community. You're the key my brothers and sisters, which is why the oppressor works overtime to keep you all divided. But, just in case you haven't heard, or you don't know, or maybe you just pretend not to know, once you find the strength to come together and start banging to uplift your community with a joint effort, it's game over. You'll change the world as we know it. It'll be Black Wall Street all over again!

For decades all we've done is bang against each other and we continue to get the same results, which is mass incarceration in prisons and graves. You've been running around in the same circle by design for far too long, and it keeps all of our communities stagnated.

You must organize yourselves and get behind your people and push!

Now's the time..........

I want to thank Lady Supreme for the time and patience; the dedication and the leg work she put in to make this book a reality. J-Pone, my brother, your support and guidance, and confidence in me gave me the strength to succeed. I couldn't have done it without you. Haze, Mars, Mantana, Cash, Blake, Ev, Fro-Gotti, Shadow, Fatal, Philly, G-Star, Monster, Loco, Ag, Bully, Lo-key,

Draco, Shy, Meatball, Miami, B-ready, Erupt-One, Chewy, Trill, Rico, Respect, Set-trip, Kutty, CeCe, C-murder, Jim Jim, Mad Dawg, Razor, Harlem-P, Tank, Tom Tom, Scrap, Mexican Mafia, MS-13, Blue-face, Sur-13, On-sight, One Hundred, Seven-30, Crazy, Rio, Tony Red, Gunz, Black, Mustafa, Pretty Paul, Killah, Beast, Rachett, Gun Smoke, D.B., Shorty Dread, Loyalty, Soldier, Burner, Ghost, Pop-off, Knuckles, Flip, D-Nice Trigg, And-#1, Killah-Bee, Red Star, Juice, Dawg Face, Shooter, Nuttsso, Dash, Purp, Pretty Tony, Smooth, Lucky, Megatron, Sun, Mike-Mike, Banks, Stacks, Big John, Big Mike, Dirty, Mann, Bishop, Sosa, Stick, K.D., Six, Biggs, L.O., Rex, Mills, Star Boy, Tati, Free, Mad Max, T-Bone, Buju, Fatt Tony… And for all you real live muthah-fuckahs that know me, and I forgot to mention you, there's no love lost. You still in my heart. Black Lives Matter supporters and all of you that are deeply involved in the social justice movement for change… We love you!!!!!

Keep pushing.

I'm your number one fan.

Author Notes

Hey, urban fans, how are you? Hopefully by the time you hold this book in your hands it will find you all blessed. My name is Tracy Lamont Davis, I'm 49 years old. For the past 28 years I have been incarcerated in North Carolina. Currently I'm serving a 90-year prison sentence for 2 counts of robbery with a dangerous weapon and one count of common law robbery, so trust me, I know all about the struggle, and how we, as a people suffer continually due to systemic racism which leads to mass incarceration. It's called oppression, and I know it like the back of my hand. I can see it coming from a mile away. I guess you're wondering how have I survived all this time in prison? It's because I'm a realist. The ultimate stand-up guy. Loyal to the core. Respectful. And trustworthy. I've written several books in the past, but I won't name them because they were stolen from me. All of my family are either dead or they don't remember me so I didn't have anyone that I could trust which caused me to take some major losses. But I didn't give up. As a matter of fact, I became stronger. I began to write with a burning desire and ambition to succeed regardless of the obstacles or the odds that were stacked against me. God blessed me. I can write 300 pages of a book in a months' time. I'm unique! All this time that I've been in prison I've been studying and educating myself. I've read thousands of books and counting.

This is not an ordinary urban novel like all the ones you're used to. In this novel it's Black Lives Matter everything, and Social Justice movement is the spotlight. I give you plenty of action, drama, and a ton of sex. But for the main course, all the people that have been killed by the cops over the past years and decades, I bring them all back to life in this book out of love and respect. Just for you.

Co-Author Bio

Hi, Urban Novel fans!! How are you? This is your girl, Kenya Moore, a.k.a. Sexy Red, sending all you readers a shout out and a heads up on the new book me and my brothers are about to drop called Black Vigilante: Thah Xah Qshunah. This book is gonna shake up the game because me and Tra and Major definitely done took this urban writing thing to another level. So, get ready to be overwhelmingly entertained. I assure you that you won't be disappointed…

First and foremost, I want to thank Allah and to my brothers Tra and Major for making this possible. I'm a 48-year-old Black Queen, a loving mother of two born and raised in New York but resides in North Carolina. To my haters, keep hating cause I'm going to keep pushing forward while ya'll still behind me…

Kenya S. Moore
A.K.A.
Sexy Red

Table of Contents

CHAPTER 1

I CAN'T BREATHE

Nine, one, one. What is your emergency?"

"Yea, there's this big black dude in the store. I think he just paid for a purchase with a counterfeit bill."

"Are you sure?"

"Yeah, I'm looking at it now. It's fake," the store clerk at the mini market replied as he began giving the dispatcher a complete description of the black man walking around in the store. Suddenly the tall black man began to sing. He smiles. He seemed very happy for some reason.

"I think he's high on something too," the clerk said.

"O.K. don't approach him or cause any type of confrontation. There's a car on the way. They should be there in less than two minutes," the dispatcher said.

"Thank you."

Outside the store two police cars pulled into the parking lot. Several police officers exited their cars and began walking towards the front of the store. The tall black man didn't notice the cops until he was opening the door of the store, getting ready to leave. He almost panicked. Instantly he remembered that he had several little baggies of meth and cocaine in his shirt pocket. Momentarily his mind wanders. He thinks about his daughter. For a split second he sees himself with this hands behind his back sitting in jail, getting ready to go back to prison again. 'I can't go back,' he tells himself as he quickly digs into his pocket and grabs the several baggies of drugs. Without missing a beat he quickly tosses the bags of dope in his mouth and swallows them. He smiles again as he thinks about his little girl and the rest of his loving family. It's time to go home. Behind him he doesn't see the store clerk motioning to the officers that he's the suspect which handed him the counterfeit bill.

As the tall black man was about to turn and head up the sidewalk, two of the cops step in front of him.

"Hey, buddy, what did you just swallow?" one of the cops asked.

"Swallowed? What the fuck you talkin bout man. I ain't swallowed shit," the tall black man said as he faced the officers.

"Put your hands behind your back, you're under arrest muthahfuckah!" the second cop said as he grabbed the black man's arm and began roughly forcing it behind his back.

"For what!?" the black man shouted as he began to struggle.

"Stop resisting. I don't want to have to tase your black ass, muthahfuckah!" the second cop says as they continued to struggle.

From out of nowhere a third cop appears and locks his arm around the black man's neck in one of those famous police choke holds that's known for killing muthahfuckahs.

The back man's air has been cut off. He can't (even) breathe in or out. Fear sets in. He tries to relax and stop struggling hoping that the third officer will loosen the grip on his neck so he can breathe. But as soon as he stops struggling they slam him to the ground face first. Different color stars flash before his eyes.

"I told you . . . . . . to stop . . . . re . . . sisting." one of the cops said as he punched the black man several times in the back of the head while gritting his teeth, breathing heavily. The cop that had his arm wrapped around his neck loosened his grip a little. The black man took in a deep breath relieved to finally get some air into his lungs. The cop that had punched him several times punched him again for the hell of it.

"Next time we tell you to do something boy, you better not give us no trouble if you know what's good for you," one of the cops said standing up and giving the black man a savage kick to the ribs.

He pissed on himself as he nearly lost consciousness. They still had him pinned to the ground pressing his face into the concrete.

A crowd of spectators began to form.

"Hey, what the hell y'all doing to that man, you already got him down?"

"Yea, what the fuck y'all doin?" someone else in the crowd yelled.

By this time, the third officer had switched positions and was now pinning the black man's neck.

"Officer, I can't breathe," the black man said. He had already told the officer that he couldn't breathe several times, but the officer ignored him.

"If you talking you can breathe," one of the cops that was kneeling on his back said sarcastically.

The crowd began to get bigger. A girl standing on the sidewalk pulled her iPhone out and began recording the incident.

The black man began to get weaker and weaker. He had told the cop that he couldn't breathe so many times that he couldn't remember.

"He can't breathe!" someone in the crowd yelled.

A bystander, who happened to be a registered nurse, happened to be walking by and saw what was going on. She looked at the man the police had pinned to the ground and to her it looked like he was barely alive.

"Let me check his vital signs officer, I'm a nurse. That man looks like he's dying," she said as she began to approach the scene.

The officer that was kneeling on the black man's neck pulled his taser out and pointed it at the nurse. She froze.

"This is police business and you're interfering in an active crime scene, if you don't step back I'm going to tase you," the officer said with a smile on his face.

The woman stepped back.

By this time it seemed like everybody had their phones out recording.

Even though no one could actually tell what he was doing, the officer leaning on the black man's neck had been slowly increasing the pressure since he first started kneeling on the man. He thought he would have been dead by now. He put his hands in his pockets and stared into the crowd of all the people who were pointing their phones at him. He even smiled for the cameras. He felt the man go limp beneath his knee and knew without a shadow of a doubt that he had just crushed the life out of him. He remembered when the man started crying out for his mother he nearly burst into uncontrollable laughter. Officer Erick Holdin was a racist muthahfuckah and he knew it. He hated niggahs, Asians, Mexicans and Jews. He wished that he could lock every last one of them up or put a bullet in their brain. God knows that he'd locked up more than his share since he'd been on the force. He actually lived for the moment. This is a white man's world and niggahs had to be kept in their place. Holdin was part of a brotherhood which existed within the Criminal Justice System since slavery. An organization which began when slave patrols and lynch mobs formed Americas first police forces. A system of terror designed to keep all non-white races subjugated. By all means necessary. Whatever the cost, blacks were to be kept in a perpetual state of fear of white authority. Where lynching was the top method of control purposes.

Officer Holdin was still staring defiantly into the crowd of spectators when the paramedics pulled up beside him and the other two officers that continued to pin the black man to the ground. One of these meddling fools must have called an ambulance Holdin thought as he and the other officers rose to their feet. The paramedics immediately went to work on the black man, checking for a pulse rate, body temperature and blood pressure. Within seconds they begin administering CPR. Moments later they were looking at the officers shaking their heads as they loaded the black man's body into the ambulance. He was dead.

Nine and a half minutes. That's how long the cop knelt on the black man's neck. There's no telling how long it actually took for the man to die but he was definitely gone.

"You think you real tuff don't you? You're a murderer . . . You fuckin coward muthahfuckah! . . . I bet you think that you're a real man now, don'tcha. . . . . Bitch ass muthahfuckah!"

"I guess y'all muthahfuckah think y'all gonah keep killing us don'tcha?"

An angry mob began to form. The word was traveling fast. Another police killing of an unarmed black man. The social media networks became overwhelmed with the images of the police killing overnight.

The angry mob quickly swelled from a hundred to a few hundred, to several thousand in less than an hour. The Rocky Mount Police Department was surrounded and overwhelmed, the people had had enough. Centuries of oppression and brutality had finally come to a head, and it was boiling over. Tensions began to flare as individuals in the crowd began throwing bricks through police car windows. Several squad cars were overturned and set on fire.

"No justice!"

"No peace!"

"No justice!"

"No peace!"

"No justice!"

"No peace!"

The chants became louder and louder as the people demanded that the officers involved in the killing of the unarmed black man be charged with murder.

Multiple police vehicles loaded with police wearing riot gear converged on the area. Minutes later they were shooting tear gas canisters into the crowd, and pepper spray.

It was total mayhem. People began picking up the canisters of tear gas and slinging them back at the police, along with bricks and anything they could get their hands on. One police officer was hit in the face with a brick, and it caved in the whole left side of his skull. Police responded with more tear gas and rubber bullets. There were loud screams and shouts coming from all directions. An old black woman was shot in the face with a rubber bullet, and it knocked her eye out. Once news spread through the crowd of what happened to the woman, people began attacking the police building and setting it on fire. Large groups of men stormed the building and released all the men and woman who were in the cell blocks of the jail before ransacking the building and setting everything that would burn on fire.

The angry crowd continued to grow.

The police were so grossly outnumbered they were forced to retreat.

The mayor declared a state of emergency and called in the National Guard.

CHAPTER 2

WAKE UP!

"Have you seen the news?"

"Naw, why. What's up?" George said, wiping the cole from his eyes.

"Looks like the police done killed another muthahfuckah."

"Say word."

"Yeah, man, shit is out of control. People been looting and setting shit on fire all night and this morning. They done called for the National guards and everything."

"Tell me something new. Ain't that what they always do when they know they done some fucked up shit to us?"

"You feel me?"

"No doubt."

"Yo, turn to CNN, they're showing the shit now," Andrew Brown said as he shifted his phone between his shoulder and his left ear so he could turn his own TV up. He and George Floyd had been friends since they were adolescents. They used to go to the same church before his grandma died. Before eventually attending the same schools. That was years ago. They were grown now. As soon as George turned the TV on and switched the channel to CNN the dramatic scene was already unfolding. Instantly the screen was filled by a police officer kneeling on a black man's neck while a crowd of onlookers shouted and screamed at the cop, telling the officer that the man on the ground couldn't breathe.

When the scene switched to a different angle George noticed the other two cops pinning the man to the ground. "Mommma!" the man on the ground being restrained by police cried out.

"You watchin it?" Andrew asked.

"Yeah," George replied eyes glued to the television. He listened as the man told the officer that he couldn't breathe so many times that he lost count. He couldn't believe what he was seeing. He became angry as he stared at the obvious lynching of an unarmed black man on national TV. Tears of rage began to drop from his eyes. His vision became blurry. His throat became so dry and sore that he couldn't even swallow. He balled-up his fist. He felt like punching something. He was so frustrated he didn't know what to do.

"George, you still there? George?"

"Yeah, I'm still here," George answered in a voice that didn't sound nothing like his own.

"That's some fucked up shit ain't it?"

"It's more than fucked up. It's sick. . . . The same shit keeps happening over and over, and over and over. These muthahfuckahs done lost their minds or something. They must think this is the god ole days, and that we're still in slavery."

"I know, right?"

"I'm talkin bout, this shit has been happening for so long that it don't make sense. Every time you turn around these muthahfuckahs killing us. . . And it's the same oh excuse. I thought he was reaching for a weapon, I thought my life was in danger, he reached for my weapon."

"Shiiit. Six months ago the white bitch said she thought she was reaching for her taser when she shot O'Boy in the chest."

"I seen that," George said as his face contracted into a mask of hatred. "Somebody gottah do something yo. If not this shit just gonah keep happening, you feel me."

"Word," Andrew said nodding his head in agreement. "What you got in mind?"

"I can't talk about it over the phone, you already know how these crackers be on the Inspector Gadget shit."

"Word, word. Say less then."

"I tell you what. I'mah swing through and pick you up in about an hour. Just give me a chance to get myself together, then we can chop it up, you feel me?"

"No doubt."

"I'mah holler back."

"One."

George set his phone down on his nightstand. He stretched back on his bed and closed his eyes. The image of the recent killing of the unarmed black man flashed before his eyes instantly. He felt his blood pressure rising. He sat up and ran his hands through his dreads. His heart was thumping so hard in his chest he could hear it. Emotions were running through his body like electrical currents. He wanted revenge. He wanted to punish the system that had oppressed his people for centuries. He was going to find a way to make them pay.

But how? He wished that he had an army. As he walked around his small apartment he began to think more and more on the matter. Before long he was obsessed with his thoughts and planning. "These muthahfuckahs need a taste of their own medicine," he mumbled to himself. "I'm tire of this shit," he said shaking his head. He was twenty-seven years old. Same age as his best friend Andrew. Tall, dark skin, brown eyes and built like a truck. Standing at six-foot, four inches he was a force to recon with, weighing in at two hundred and thirty pounds solid. Most dudes knew not to fuck with him and those who didn't found out the hard way. He was well known in the hood. Never one to start shit but didn't shy away when it was time to get down and dirty. He was respected. Ran with a crew of real brothers and some real live chicks that was bout that life. Andrew, Daunte, Fred, Eric, Breonna, Trayvon and Ahmaud were his number one Road Doggs. These were people that he'd been through the trenches with. They grew up together. Without a second thought he would trust his life with anyone of them. they were solid. The type of muthahfuckahs you would want having your back when it was time to go to war. In some way or another they'd all been together since they were knee high to a baby. And they all looked up to George like he was the leader of their pack. He was definitely smart and intelligent. And above all he was loyal. He was a thinker. Calm. Never quick to jump to any conclusions. Straight up. And always about his business. You couldn't ask for a better friend.

George jumped in the shower as he continued to ponder the subject in his mind. A fire was burning within him. Seeing one of his people just die like that caused something to snap inside him. Every time he recalled the scene the rage in him would rise. All the books he read about slavery, racism, and discrimination were all suddenly being broadcast from a very loudspeaker in his mind. He couldn't turn the images off. Nor did he want to. He embraced every thought of every conceivable act of violence that could be concocted against a century's old archenemy.

"This is the hate that hat created," he said . . .

"This sis the hate that hate created!" he screamed at the top of his lungs!

He turned the water off and exited the shower. It was time to get ready. He was a man on a mission.

****

"Yesterday another black man was lynched. Michael Brown became yet another victim of the long running graphic acts of systemic hate and racism in this country. A statistic added to the list of a State Sponsored Police brutality and injustices, where his only crime was the color of his skin. A tragic event which we all witnessed, which has plagued our nation for centuries.

When will it end?

What will it take?

How many more of us have to die in these streets or these prisons before the white man will recognized us as human beings?

We were brought to this country against our will. Kidnapped! Our women were raped. Our children were molested. Our men were tortured for hundreds and hundreds of years.

They say in 1865 the slaves were set free, but when I look around all I can see is the same oh oppressor. How can we possibly be free when we're under the same laws and rulership of those who enslaved us for centuries? How were we freed from our chains when there's ten times more black men, women and children than there were slaves during slavery in prison. How can we be free when our men, women and children are sitting in prison serving genocidal sentences being imposed by the same people who committed every act of crime known to man against us for more than three hundred years, and didn't do a single day in jail for it? Somebody tell me, how are we free.

If we were truly free Michael Brown would be alive today and among us.

Something ain't right yet. Maybe I'm missing something, but to me America don't live up to its promise.

They call us criminals!

Now ain't that something. The same people that exterminated the Indians with cannon balls and built an empire off the exploitation of people of color are now the lilliest white muthah-fuckahs in the world. And the champions against crime.

Come on y'all. What's really going on?

And since we on the subject of crime let's talk about where crime comes from, or rather where it came from.

For those of you that don't know, this is how you learned how to commit crimes, it came from watching the white man and woman rape, kidnap and murder us for centuries. It came from watching the white man and woman molest our men, women and children. It came from watching them steal our land and resources. They robbed us. Highjacked all our inventions. I hope y'all paying attention because here's the catch.

Any race or group of people that goes hundreds of years without learning how to read or write, or without obtaining any type of knowledge or education will mimic everything they see and hear around them.

This is why we think, talk and act like white people today.

What did you think that they were doing when they kept you from learning how to read or write for hundreds of years? But hold up, I'm not finished. I want to make sure that y'all take all of this in, you feel me?

Now when you wake up in the morning don't think that you're the smartest muthahfuckah in the world, or that you all the way up on your shit because you're not, because over ten thousand years of your forefathers ancient history has been erased from your memory. You can't speak your own language, nor do you know your true history or culture.

And for those of you who don't know, the true power of your mind, the mind is so powerful that what you think of habitually your mind creates. See these white folks know us better than we know ourselves. They've been studying us.

You may ask well how does crime continue to plague our communities?

Through T.V radio and the mass media. They know that if they can get you to think about it long enough that your mind will create it.

These muthahfuckahs are going to make the best gangsta movies and songs in the world because they know that it'll produce crime.

We been sleeping and we gottah wake up.

We're weak minded and scared.

They say they're not really worried about us because we've been so systematically programmed with fear of the system that the most we'll ever do is march in the street or burn and loot a few buildings, hold hands and sing "We Shall Overcome" but other than that we're no real threat to the system.

Tell me something, when y'all gonnah be tired of being sick and tired!

It's time for action."

The crowd began to chant "Black Lives Matter," "No Justice No Peace," at the huge rally taking place on Ravenwood in Rocky Mount, North Carolina. There was so many people out there that one could barely move.

The people were standing together in solidarity, and it was about damn time. George was taking it all in. he was paying close attention. When he heard about the rally that was being held he knew he and his crew had to be there.

"That brother said some powerful words. A lot of shit he was talking about, I didn't even know that," Breonna said.

"Me either. They sure didn't tell us no shit like that in our history class," Eric replied.

"Shiiit, it's so much shit that they've kept from us you wouldn't believe," Fred said.

"Oh I would believe," she said.

"Me too."

"I'm still trippin off the fact of how they kilt that boy like that."

"I know, right?"

"They didn't give a fuck either, right, on National television."

"You feel me. I guess that's their way of saying Hey look world this is what we do to niggahs in America," Trayvon said mean mugging.

"I wonder how they'll like it if we start doing them like that," Ahmaud said.

"Word."

George was listening. It was clear that they all felt the same way. How far would they be willing to go was the question.

It was a beautiful day in March, clear bule skies, sun shining bright. There was so many people out there it seemed hard to believe that there was a global pandemic ravaging the world.

"Fuck social distancing huh?"

"it is what it is."

"We out here," Daunte said.

"I'm down for the cause."

"Me too."

They all shook their heads in agreement.

"Are y'all really down for the cause or are y'all just caught up in the moment?" George asked.

"What do you mean?" Breonna said. She turned and faced him. He looked at her. She was beautiful, short, thick, pretty brown skin, little feet, sweet sounding voice, pretty brown eyes, luscious full lips, tiny waist with more ass than Pinky. A five star chick no question. But niggahs better not get it twisted. She could be lady-like but can turn into a gangsta bitch whenever she felt like flippin the switch.

"I'm talking about retribution. Y'all see what's going on. And it ain't like these muthahfuckahs just started doing this shit. I been hearing about this shit since we were kinds. They pop all muthahfuckah and all we do is march up and down the street, holding up picket signs and taking up our own neighborhoods. That's it. Ain't nobody clappin back. If ah muthahfuckah know you ain't gonah do shit if they kill your ass what you think they gon do? They gon ah keep killin your ass, which is exactly what these muthahfuckahs been doing. They've kilt thousands and thousands of our people over the past two hundred years, guess how many cops have went to prison for it"

"How many?" Breonna asked.

"Seven," he said.

"You bullshittin," Daunte said, in disbelief.

"I wish," George said.

They all had a sour expression on their faces. Fred kept shuffling his feet back and forth. He was definitely not happy about what he'd just heard. None of them were.

"We need to go somewhere where we can talk about this," Andrew said.

"We can go to my crib," George said.

"It's official then. We'll meet up at Georges crib after the rally's over," Trayvon said.

"That's what's up."

Everybody shook their head in agreement. The things that the brothers and sisters were talking about when they took the podium took on a more elevated meaning to them. they listened closely to every word as the cries against systemic racism and injustices in America increased their anxiety.

"Wake up black people! Don't be afraid to stand up for your rights. We must all shake off our fears and come together for this common cause. We've been oppressed for far too long. Who can we turn to? Who's gonah save us? Who can protect us from this mighty oppressor? Who's willing to defy this centuries old oppressor/ They say the most potent weapon in the hands of the oppressor is the minds of the oppressed. But I'm here to tell you today that those psychological chains of slavery are broken, and we refuse to be killed in these streets any longer.

Stand up! Unify yourselves! Protect your communities! Make a better world for our children. This is a call to action! . . . .

CHAPTER 3

PRESS RELEASE

"The officers involved in the incident concerning the death of Michael Brown have been placed on paid leave pending an investigation," said Police Chief Clinton Sumner as he took the podium and began the press conference.

"Chief Sumner will the officers be charged with murder?", a reporter from WRAL asked.

"I'm not at liberty to say right now due to the ongoing investigation."

"Chief Sumner, there's been massive protests in the black communities calling for justice, have you spoke to any members of the community?"

"We have, and we've asked them to stay calm and allow the justice process to complete its inquiry. A full investigation will be conducted with transparency."

A short redheaded reporter from Fox News raised her hand. "Yes."

"Chief Sumner, what is the Police Department doing to combat the looting and rioting that's been recently taking place?"

"Let me be clear. We vigorously denounce any acts of violence, and we will do our job in maintaining law and order to keep our communities and properties safe. We encourage peaceful protests."

"But Chief Sumner, isn't it true that many of these protests have already become violent?"

"Yes. Also, arrests have been made and those who have broken the law will be prosecuted," chief Sumner replied. He hated the press with their stupid questions. Sometimes he wished that he could smack a few of them around and teach them some respect, and not to question authority. This was already turning into a long day, and he couldn't wait to get back to his office and pour himself a tall glass of bourbon. The way things were going he had a good feeling that he wouldn't be getting a break anytime soon.

"Chief Sumner, according to reports there's been calls from the public for the city and the police to be more tougher on protesters, how will your department respond?"

"We do not want to incite people to commit more violence or escalate more tensions. There's already enough tension. If people are insinuating that we violate people's constitutional rights, no, we're not going to even consider that. But we're certainly not going to allow people to vandalize and destroy our community either." Even as he spoke there were more protests being held around the country. Accordingly, the mayor announced a curfew from 11:00 PM Sunday until 6:00 AM Monday saying that it would allow protesters the right to assemble while also helping to protect area residents and businesses. But so far nothing was actually safe. Where the protesters went, they left a message for injustice in the form of destructions, vandalism, and carnage. The greatest rise against the criminal justice system and white supremacy had begun.

CHAPTER 4

THE HATE THAT HATE CREATED

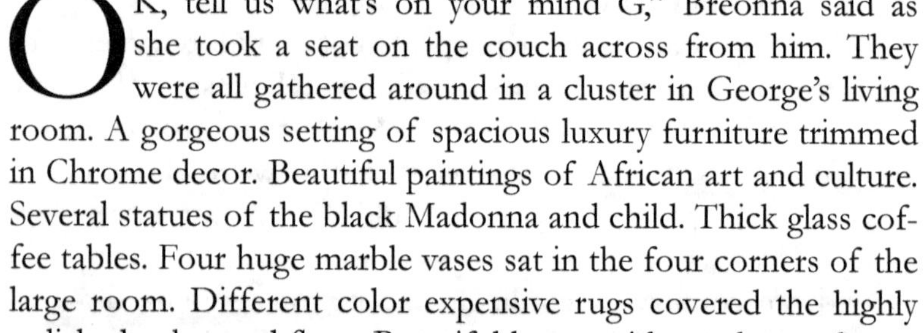

"OK, tell us what's on your mind G," Breonna said as she took a seat on the couch across from him. They were all gathered around in a cluster in George's living room. A gorgeous setting of spacious luxury furniture trimmed in Chrome decor. Beautiful paintings of African art and culture. Several statues of the black Madonna and child. Thick glass coffee tables. Four huge marble vases sat in the four corners of the large room. Different color expensive rugs covered the highly polished oak wood floor. Beautiful lamps with parchment lampshades of all colors were perfectly placed about the room. A TV so big it looked like a projector screen took up the far wall, surrounded by this state-of-the-art entertainment system.

"Nice place," Daunte said looking around admiring the room.

"Yeah, man, you got a tight ass crib," Ahmaud said, digging in his pocket and pulling out five boxes of cigars and an ounce of loud.

"Damn that shit smell good," Trayvon said, reaching for one of the boxes of cigars.

"Mind if we smoke?," Ahmaud said, licking one of the cigars.

George got up and grabbed a couple of Chrome ashtrays that were sitting on the nightstand. "Please Be my guest. Pass that shit, light that shit, smoke it," George said smiling, "I got some gin and some honey in the fridge, y'all trin' tah get fucked up tonight," he asked.

"Hell, yeah!," Breonna said smiling. Andre and Fred helped pour everybody drinks. Eric came back from the kitchen carrying a bucket filled with ice.

Everybody got relaxed. George turned on some sounds.

"Now tell us what you were talking about earlier," Breonna said, taking her shoes off and pulling her legs up under her on the couch.

"Alright. Yo. Everybody power your phones off and hand them to me," George said.

"Why, what's up?," Eric asked.

"Let's just say, I believe in Big Brother's capabilities, you feel me?"

They all looked a little skeptical but nevertheless they all turned their phones off and handed it to him. George placed all the phones in a plastic container, took them to the kitchen and placed them in the refrigerator. He returned to the living room moments later.

"I can hear my girl now, 'Who you been fuckin, Why you had your phone off?,'" Fred said.

"You ain't the only one," Trayvon said.

"Tell 'em you was with me. I'm sure I can cover for you if it comes to that." George said.

"Y'all niggahs got babysitters, y'all ain't pimp[in, you dudes are part timers," Ahmaud said grinning, taking a long pull on his blunt and blowing the smoke at them.

"Shut up fool. That's why you ass stay at the clinic, you dirty dick muthahfuckah." Fred said.

Breonna started cracking up. The weed was starting to kick in.

Ahmaud gave them the middle finger. He took another deep pull on his blunt.

"How y'all feel about what's been going on recently with these cop killings?" George asked.

"Recently! You mean continually don't chah? It ain't never stopped. This shit been going on forever," Trayvon said.

"As long as I can remember these crackers been poppin niggahs tops and getting away with it," Andrew said with a scold.

"Word. They just killed a little boy in Shy-Town not too long ago."

"And Oh-Boy had his hands up right?"

"Yeah."

"That's some fucked up shit."

"Word up."

"Somebody needs to stop these clowns."

"These muthahfuckahs is out of order."

"I know, right."

"Muthahfuckahs ain't gonah do shit. They scared to death. All they gonah do is walk up and down the street, waving a bunch of signs singing "Swing low Sweet Chariot," Eric said with obvious disdain.

"Real talk. But they'll be quick to kill one another, you feel me? I don't get it. Muthahfuckahs ah kill each other but they won't do shit to the oppressor. This shit crazy as hell," Daunte said, a frustrated expression on his face.

"It pisses me off, Yo."

"You ain't the only one," Breonna said. "If muthahfuckahs start lighting their ass up they'll think twice about doin that shit," she said rolling her eyes.

"That's why I asked y'all to come here," George said.

"What do you mean?"

"I mean it's time to join the revolution. Stop talking about and be about it. You feel me? Do you know how it makes me feel every time I see that mother or that grandmother on TV crying because one of these bitchass muthahfuckahs dun took their son's or their daughter's life? I've been feeling that same pain yo for real. I can't even sleep because I've been thinking about that shit so much. And I keep saying why ain't nobody doing nothing. You got all these muthahfuckahs running around claiming they gang-stas, but they won't buss their gun at the muthahfuckahs that's been killing them for centuries," George said.

"That's some real shit. I be feeling the exact same way some-times. You claim you bang against oppression but all you do is bang against your own people and communities," Fred said. "They got it twisted."

"Fools."

"Just look back over the last ten years alone. The police have really killed a whole lot of us."

"Thousands."

"And what really makes it so bad is that the police as we know them today came from slave patrols, lynch mobs, and Klu Klux Klans," Trayvon said.

"That ain't even the half of the story because when slavery supposedly ended crackers started building courts, jails and pris-ons like crazy. They took us from chattel-slavery to convict leas-ing system, to prison system, to the department of corrections, to the department of public safety. They tricked us. Remember what the brother said at the rally? They taught us all these crimes by committing them against us for centuries with impunity." George said.

"Impunity? What does that mean?" Ahmaud asked.

"It means they were not punished for a single act of crime they committed against us," Breonna said.

"Lynchin niggahs, raping women and little kids, cutting muthahfuckahs hands and feets off. All that shit was legal for them. Now our people are sitting up in prisons with millions of years," Erick said.

"That's some bullshit."

"And it ain't just these crackers, these house niggahs still sup-porting em."

"They can get it too."

"No doubt."

"Same way I kill ah white cop I'll kill ah niggah cop too."

"Out the gate."

"Word up."

"Ah nigga cop, ah niggah judge, ah nigga D.A., ah nigga prison guard, anybody that's a part of the system of the oppression of our people is in my crosshairs," Trayvon said pretending like he was aiming a gun at a target.

"Word up."

"So what y'all tryin' tah say?" Y'all tryin tah go ta war wit the oppressor?"

"It's been ah war. The only one that's been shooting is them, we the ones that's been thinking shit's ah game."

"Y'all niggah's off the chain in here," Breonna said.

"Don't get scared now bitch!," Ahmaud said.

"Niggah I ain't scared. And I ain't your bitch. Matter fact, you see ah bitch smack ah bitch," she said pulling a long razor blade from somewhere. She hopped up off the couch.

"Yo, chill out yo, the enemy ain't up in here you feel me?," George said.

"Word. Y'all need to squash that shit."

"No doubt."

"Word up."

"Y'all niggah better tighten up."

"I'm just sayin yo, niggah's ain't gonah be disrespecting me like that, hump," Breonna said rolling her eyes at Ahmaud. She put the razor blade up.

Ahmaud stood up. He walked over to her. She had her arms folded across her chest, still rolling her eyes.

"I'm sorry Ma," he leaned in and grabbed her and started kissing her all over her face.

"ILLLL, your breath stank. Get this niggah off of me," she cried, trying to push him away.

Everybody started laughing.

Ahmaud smacked her on the butt and grabbed himself a handful. She started punching him and trying to knee him in the nuts. The tension was gone just like that. Everybody was still laughing.

"Alright y'all, lets continue addressing this matter y'all heard," George said as he began rolling another blunt.

"Yo, how we gonah fight these muthahfuckahs, they got all the guns, all the bombs, all the tanks, all the planes. . . . . "

"Guerilla warfare. Assassins creed," Trayvon said in a haunting voice.

"Exactly. We know that we can't confront them head on, so we catch them slippin and we push their wigs back. When we go hunting, we dress up in different disguises and we retaliate. We work as a team. One, two and three-man teams."

"Two men and one woman," Breonna added.

"Is there anybody who don't want to get involved in this? Speak now or forever hold your peace. Because what we're about to do takes a lot of heart. It's a seriously bold move that takes courage," George said.

"If you ain't living for something that ain't worth dying for you ain't living. You frontin."

"We gonnah die one day anyway," Breonna said.

"I rather die on my feet than die on my knees."

"Ain't nobody else standing up, we mightest well set the trend you feel me."

"Show these muthahfuckahs what real ganstas do. Word up," Daunte said.

"They dun got too comfortable. They must have been under the impression that centuries-old fear tactic was gonah work forever."

"Fools."

"They should of known this day was coming. We gave em over four centuries to learn how to love us and they still hated."

"Get ready to meet the Black Vigilantes muthahfuckahs."

CHAPTER 5

SOUNDS LIKE A PLAN

"We need money, and we need guns, and we need lots of both of them, any suggestions?" George asked.

"We could sell drugs."

"We could rob a bank."

"How bout we kidnap somebody rich for a ransom."

"I say we rob a couple big drug dealers."

George was in deep thought as he listened to their plots. Every option was on the table and open for consideration.

"I'm sure there's somebody out there that's rich, that would love to donate to our cause," Breonna said.

"You're right. But who?"

"What's the biggest organization out there right now that's leading the charge against police killings and police brutality?"

It didn't take them long to come up with that answer.

"Black lives matter!"

"Well, you got a few NBA players and NFL's that be voicing their opinions."

"Them niggahs drunk on the white man's money, we tell them muthahfuckahs what we're about to do and their liable to call the cops personally, you feel me?"

"You better not tell Charles Backley, that's for sure," Trayvon said.

"I think we should run down on that chick that dun made all this money off the people."

"You talking about Oh Girl from Black lives matter?"

"Yeah."

"I agree."

"Me too."

"I like the sound of that. And if that don't work we'll go to plan B and C."

"And what's that?"

"Robbery and kidnapping."

Andrew was shaking his head.

"What?," George asked.

"I don't like it. It's not a good plan," Andrew said.

"Why not? What's wrong with it?"

"One, it's too risky, this chick got millions of people in the streets marching, you best believe the FED's are already watching her. We liable to expose ourselves just by approaching her you feel me? And two, we can't afford to tell anyone outside this circle what we planning to do. Are you crazy? We already bout to do some shit that'll have our black asses waring a red jumpsuit. We damn sure can't afford to let ah muthahfuckah we don't even know have that kind of information unless you planning on killing em on the spot. We gottah stay low as possible. We gottah move like ghost," Andrew said.

Everybody paused. They let everything he was saying sink in.

"Yo Drew right yo. We really can't afford to let nobody know nothing or it'll be over before it gets started. These muthahfuckahs be out here snitchin so much the muthahfuckahs you think ain't snitchin, snitchin," Eric said.

"No doubt."

"So what we gonah do then? It's definitely going to take money to fund this mission. There's no question about that."

"We do what we do best."

"And what's that?"

"We sell drugs," Andrew said. "It ain't like we ain't did it before. All we need is a couple of months and we should have enough to get started. It's a whole lot safer and nobody will ever have a clue to what we are up to."

"Sounds like a plan," George said.

"Well, I got a connect on the pills," Breonna said.

"My man in Wilson pushin mad weed. I know I can get him to front me some weight," Fred said.

"I still fuck wit Clyde down south he got shit on smash with the coke; he been trying to get me to hustle for him," Andrew stated.

"Everybody know Meatball. That niggah probably sitting on millions fuckin wit that Ron. Matter fact when y'all brought it up, that's who I thought about robbing. My cousin sell weight for him. I'm sure I can get him to put my foot in the door," Ahmaud said, digging in his pocket and pulling out some more weed.

"Eric, Daunte, Trayvon, we need y'all to find a good trap spot and set up shop."

"I already got something in mind," Trayvon said.

"Me too," Daunte echoed.

"While we're doing all this, what you gonah be doing?" Ahmaud asked.

Everybody turned and looked at George. George smiled wickedly.

"ME? Shiiiit, I'm ah be killing my first cop to prove to y'all I'm down for the cause and willing to go to war for my people," he said.

"It's official then. Let's all meet back here in one week and report on our progress."

"That's what's up."

"Let's move then."

Three days later around 8:30 PM it had just turned dark. George had been looking for the perfect set up when he decided to test his luck and see if the rumor was true. "They say cops like dunking coffee and eating donuts." He was dressed like a bum in some baggy brown checkerboard pin stripe pants, a beige turtleneck sweater with several holes in it and grease stains. He had a wig on that was completely grey and he walked with a fake limp. He had dirt smeared on his hands and forehead. He also had on his Covid-19 face mask. He was limping down the sidewalk towards Dunkin Donuts when he spotted them. Two cop cars, one facing in his direction, the other facing in the opposite direction. They were having a nice little chat, enjoying their nightly cup of Tasters Choice. They didn't even see him coming.

George's adrenaline was pumping so hard he thought he was about to have a heart attack or shit on himself. He kept checking his surroundings as he got closer and closer. He already knew how he was gonah do it. It was a split second decision., the weight of the nine millimeter Glock up under his sweater suddenly felt heavier and more deadlier. He was fully aware of its presences. He took a deep breath and tried to calm himself as much as possible. He couldn't. He was shaking so bad he could hear his teeth chattering like he was freezing. He stepped between the two cars like he was only focused on heading into the donut shop. Quickly he turned with the Glock in his hand and shot the first cop in the head. Brains splattered the windshield and the passenger window. Blood mixed with brain matter and bone fragments began to drip slowly down the glass. Before the other cop could think about reacting he shot him in the mouth, which was full of chocolate donut. Brains, part of the back of the cops skull, and chocolate donut went every fuckin where. It look like somebody painted the car with blood, brain matter and Dunkin Donuts. He didn't miss a beat. George limped back the way he came and disappeared into the night like a phantom. It took him about two minutes to make it back to the dirt road path where he left his four-wheeler. He was still breathing harder than ah muthahfuck-ah as he stepped into the wooded area and began stripping off the wig and the clothes he was wearing, which he stuffed in a trash bag and tucked under the seat of the four-wheeler. He took the bar of soap that he had in his boot out and slung it as far as he could.

Jumping on the four-wheeler, George kicked it to life and raised the hell up out of there. He wanted to put as much distance between himself and the crime scene as possible. He knew, the dirt path like the back of his hand. When they were kids this is where they rode their bikes all the time. He turned off the main dirt path and hit the cut. That's when he first heard the sounds of the approaching sirens. He was already long gone. He never looked back. He was almost home. Coming out of the cut he finally turned on his single head light and punched it. He drove the four-wheeler down the street like it was a motorcycle. Two blocks away from his house he finally began to relax a little, but the adrenaline was still pumpin. Jumping the curb he drove down a short gravel path to the big two-story house his grandfather left him when he passed away. He drove around to the back of the house and pulled the four-wheeler into the shed. Killing the engine, he jumped off the four-wheeler, grabbed the bag of clothes from up under the seat, then closed the shed's door. He placed the padlock on the door and locked it. Grabbing a small key from under the flowerpot next to the back door of his house he inserted the key in the lock and let himself in. For a second in is mind's eye he saw cops running from everywhere yelling freeze while pointing guns at his head. For a minute he didn't even realize that he was holding his breath. He opened up the refrigerator, grabbed a half a blunt out of the butter holder and fired it up. He picked up the half a bottle of gin from the side slot, twisted the cap off and took a long swig. He welcomed the burning sensation in his guts. He took another swig. "That's better," He said to himself. Grabbed a pair of scissors from a cabinet drawer, picked up the bag of clothes that he'd worn as a disguise, then headed to the bathroom. He sat on the edge of the bathtub then lifted the seat on the toilet. Opening up the bag, he pulled out the pants first. Slowly he began to clip up the pants in tiny pieces and flushed them down the toilet until they were gone. He picked up the sweater and did the same thing. He looked at the gun sitting on the bathroom sink. He wasn't taking any chances. Grabbing his car keys, he jumped in his car and headed toward the lake. Everything was pretty quiet like he expected. Wiping his finger-prints off the gun one more time, he slung that muthahfuckah as far as he could and listened to the distant splash. It was like a weight had just been lifted off of his chest. Carefully he pulled off the latex gloves he had on and dropped them in a waste basket on his way back to his car.

Pulling back into his driveway he noticed a car in his entrance. He almost shitted on himself again until he recognized who's car was. It was Breonna's. She was sitting on his front porch.

"What's up?"

"I saw something on the news I was worried."

He placed his finger over his lips motioning for her to be quiet. He began motioning again asking her where her phone was. She pulled it out of her pocket. Then she remembered how paranoid he was about the phones. She turned it off and they went inside.

"Two cops were killed tonight at –"

"Dunkin Donuts," he finished. "I just shot one in the head and the other in the mouth. Bre, I never been so scared before in my life. I was literally shaking in my boots." She came closer. He wrapped his arms around her and held her tight. The softness of her body cause him to form an erection so hard it hurt. She felt it rubbing against her. The lights were still off, they hadn't bothered to turn them on. She stroked his length through his pants. She had such overwhelming admiration for him. He felt her tiny little hand groping and pulling on his hardness. Suddenly his zipper was being pulled down and one of those little hands was inside his pants searching for something. A split moment later her pretty soft, luscious mouth was all over him. Instantly he began to groan as she repeatedly sunk him into her mouth letting the head of the dick hit the back of her throat.

"Goddamn this dick so big," she said as she continued to swallow him. She moaned while continuing to down him. Picking her up, he carried her upstairs to his bedroom. Quickly they undressed. Climbing onto the bed she inserted herself into the doggie style passion, face down ass up. A whole lot of ass. He climbed on the bed behind her. He was so anxious and excited; the recent drama still had him pumped. He guided himself into her folds and plunged forward.

"IIaaaaaaiiah," she cried when she felt the long black dick fill her insides to the brim. It was so good she was already starting to have her first orgasm. George stabbed forward again plowing his entire length into her. Breonna cried out again in pleasure. She lay down on her stomach as George continued to rise and fall on her with his sword repeatedly. Over and over again. Breonna moaned and whimpered with lustful glee.

CHAPTER 6

WE UP. THEY DOWN.

Our top story this morning;

"Police are searching for a man who shot and killed two Rock Mount Sheriff Deputies last night in the parking lot of a Dunkin Donuts on Raleigh Road. The police say that the suspect is a black male in his late or early fifties about six-feet tall with grey hair. The suspect was last seen fleeing the scene on foot towards the lower business district between nine and nine-thirty last night. Anyone with information that can help lead to an arrest in the shooting are asked to immediately call the Rock Mount Police Department or Crime Stoppers.

"This was a cowardly and horrible senseless act of violence. And we at the Rocky Mount Police Department vow to bring the perpetrator to justice," Rocky Mount Police Chief Clinton Sumner told reporters in an interview outside his home in Gold Rock.

"Law enforcement officials have been combing the area looking for any clues that might lead to arrests. So far they've come up empty handed as the current investigation continues.

"Surveillance footage from police dash Cam shows this man who the police believed to be the shooter, fleeing the scene after the officers were reportedly shot and killed. So far police have been unable to identify the suspect who was wearing a mask during the time of the incident.

"Once again, the police are asking the public to contact the Rocky Mount Police Department if they have any information in regard to the shooting.

"As more details surrounding the shooting unfold, you can follow us on these Fox News stations," said the news reporter sounding off.

"Oh shit, G, you ah fuckin mad man boy. You done fucked around and made history. You all fool," Andrew said smiling and giving him a hug.

Everybody gave him a hug and patted him on the back. Breonna gave him a hug and kissed him on the cheek. They'd been fuckin all night and this morning. When he hugged her something stirred within him.

"Now that's what you call some gangsta shit," Ahmaud said.

"Word up."

Daunte just looked at George, repeatedly nodding his head in admiration. His respect for the man overwhelmingly increased.

"Yo sun, that was some real niggah shit, I gottah tip my hat to you. you took one for the team," Trayvon said.

"Hell, naw, that niggah took two for the team you feel me," Fred said laughing.

"No doubt."

"This calls for a celebration," Ahmaud said, pulling out several boxes of Philly's Blunts and two ounces of weed.

"Drinks on me," Eric said. He went to this car and came back with two gallons of Gin. He was smiling.

"Gon turn that music up, we bout'tah get fucked up in here. . . Let's party yo!," Breonna said as she started dancing and shaking her hips. She had a huge grin on her face.

"I'd like to make a toast," Daunte said, "To George Floyd! The reincarnation of George Jackson," he said holding up his glass.

"To George Floyd, the reincarnation of George Jackson," they repeated.

"Power to the people! The revolution has begun."

"If you ain't beamin-up or shootin-up you gottah get the fuck-up out'ah here. This ah trap house, not ah out-house you feel me? We getting this paper in here yah-heard? If you ain't spending no cash show me your ass when door hit'cha in the back of your pants," Trayvon said smiling as he counted stacks of money he had lined up on a table in the living room of the small apartment that they had rented out for a few months.

They were trappin on Stallin Way in South Rocky Mount down the street from a nightclub called Morgan's. This was a hot spot where the money flow was frequent and constant. If you had some dope it was gonna get sold, no question. They had everything up in that, muthahfuckah, weed, coke, pills, heroin, you name it they had it. Them boys was on a mission. They wasn't out here in these streets for the fame and glory and turning a crack rock into a mountain. This was about funding a war. The oppressor had killed our people for far too long and gotten away with it, now it was time for 'em to meet the Grim Reaper. It was time for a little payback. That eye for an eye thing they be talking about. Tooth for a tooth.

Eric stood in one corner with a AR-15 pointed at the floor. Daunte stood in another corner with an AK-47 pointed at the ceiling. The plan was if anybody kicked their door in, especially the police, they was gonnah lite that muthahfuckah up to the sky.

They'd been pumping out of the house for nearly a month strong now and they had stacked up nearly one-hundred thousand dollars to the good. Everybody that fronted them some work had been paid back what they were owed. They were re-ing-up with their own money now, and everything was going accordingly.

There was a knock on the door. A special knock. The code that they gave the crackhead name "Tiny Bit" to let them know that everything was good.

Daunte raised the AK and pointed it at the door just in case the niggah had sold them out. He didn't trust anybody. He'd been in the streets long enough to know how the game go.

A crackhead chick named Jackie and her friend, another crackhead chick named Bee, came in. Both of them was thick as hell. They looked good. It was hard to believe that they smoked. Jackie sat down on the couch; she gave another crack head that was working the customers forty dollars. His name was Joe. One of the most loyalist crackheads the world has ever seen. Joe passed Trayvon the two twenty dollar bills. Trayvon gave him a bolder, which he gave to Jackie who immediately pulled out her personal pipe and went to work.

Bee kept looking at Trayvon smiling shyly. Trayvon got up from the table he was sitting at and walked down the hall to the bathroom.

"Yo com'ere Bee," Trayvon called.

Bee sassayed her way to the bathroom. She walked in. Trayvon shut the door. Immediately she got on her knees and reached for the zipper on Trayvon's pants. Her fumbling instantly aroused him. Finally she found what she was digging for. She smiled as she began pulling up and down on his shaft. Moments later she was deep throating him, making choking sounds every time it went down her throat.

Trayvon was a young freak. He liked Bee. Every time she came through he made sure she sucked his dick. Suddenly he pulled out of her mouth making that popping sound. He dug in his pocket, pulled out a condom and put it on. Bee smiled. She already knew what time it was. She turned around and pulled her pants and panties down. A bit fat, stupid looking ass greeted him.

Trayvon bent her over. He stuck the head in her pussy real slow. Bee moaned. He pulled it out and stuck the head of his dick in her asshole. She tensed. He stuck it in a little bit more. She whimpered. He'd never done that before.

"Please," she cried. She tried to move away.

Suddenly without warning Trayvon grabbed her firmly by her hips and shoved his dick into her tight little asshole. Everybody in house heard Bee hollering and moaning. Eric and Daunte started shaking their heads. Everybody that was getting high went back to getting high.

"Just another regular day at the trap house you feel me. Sex, money and drugs," Daunte said.

They could still hear Bee in the bathroom moaning.

"That niggah in there getting his Mr. Marcus on ain't he?," Ikkie said as he prepared to stick a needle in his right arm.

"Sure sounds like he putting on a good show."

"Sounds so good it's making my dick hard," another crack head named Paul said as he held a lighter to his crack pipe and inhaled a huge cloud of smoke. His eyes got big as fifty cent pieces as the crack rock sizzled on the stem. He started sucking his lips like he was tasting something. He held the smoke in as long as he could then blew it out slowly. Paul looked around the room like he was in a trance, and couldn't remember where he was, or who he was. Then slowly a huge smile spread across his face, showing a mouth full of tobacco stained teeth. "Yo y'all niggah's got some good shit. Let me get another one," he said pulling a wrinkled up fifty dollar bill out of his pocket.

Joe grabbed the money out of Paul's outstretched hand and gave it to Daunte. Daunte smoothed the bill out and placed it on the stack of bills on the table, grabbed a crack rock, which was about a half a gram and handed it to Joe.

There was another knock at the door. Daunte levelled the assault rifle. Tiny Bit peeked his head in, then ushered another customer through the door. Trayvon exited the bathroom. A few minutes later Bee came out. She was walking kind of stiffly. Trayvon waved her over to the table and handed her a nice slab. She sat down on the couch next to Jackie who looked like she'd been floating on a cloud for a week. As soon as she sat down she winced a little, her bottom was really sore.

Pulling out her pipe, Bee broke a little piece off of her slab and fired up. As soon as she took that first hit she forgot all about the pain in her ass. she didn't even notice the knowing stares she was getting. She was high. High as hell.

Eric looked at Trayvon and rolled his eyes, he shook his head.

"What?," Trayvon said, playing innocent.

"Niggah, you off the chain. Why the hell you got that girl back there hollarin like that?," Daunte said.

"We been stuck up in this muthahfuckah all day. Ain't nothing wrong with having a little fun."

"Sounds like you was having a lot of fun, that's for sure."

Trayvon had that big shit eatin grin on his face.

"Trick," Erick said, looking at Trayvon disapprovingly.

"Don't hate, congratulate. You fake, I motivate," Trayvon said smiling.

There was another knock at the door. Business was starting to pick up again.

"Somebody farted or something? Smells like somebody shitted on theyself. Damn, spray some incense up in this muthahfuckah," Paul said before taking another hit. His eyes took on that glassy look. He smiled.

CHAPTER 7

GET YOU MIND RIGHT

As the money was rolling in, the first thing they bought was chappahs. Five M-4's and two more AR-15's, all equipped with hundred round drums. They also bought a fifty caliber assault rifle with a scope on it, which came with a suppressor and an infrared beam.

They found a connect on the weapons at Fort Bragg through a big Mexican drug dealer Meatball introduced Ahmaud to. They ended up spending about two-hundred thousand dollars on guns and all types of military equipment. Walkie talkies, bullet proof vest, grenades. The Mexican even threw in a couple of ounces of C-4 and showed them how to set the timers, and how it should be stored. They were ready to rock'n'roll.

They started going to the gun range. Within a few weeks' time they could hit anything from damn near anywhere. Whereas it took crackers months and years to become excellent marksman, it came to them like something naturally.

Breonna put on a disguise and went and rented out a storage space where they kept everything. Even though she only weighed about one-hundred fifty pounds she looked like she weighed two-hundred fifty. She also looked and sounded like somebody's grandmother . . . .

"Let's go over some key issues in regard to what we're doing because there's no question that there's no room for mistakes you feel me? We gottah be perfect. Every move we make has to be made with as much accuracy as possible because one false move and it's o'vah for y'all," George said.

They were all sitting at the kitchen table with a huge stack of money in the center. A little over five-hundred thousand to be exact. Three and a half months after they started selling drugs their capital was sufficient enough for them to chill. It was time to focus more attention on the business at hand.

"Number one, don't get caught. If you get caught in a position where you can't get away, gon put the gun to your head and pull the trigger or bang out to you empty the clip. No matter what don't let 'em take you alive. Ain't no need sitting up in prison in your red jumpsuit waiting for these crackers to turn the gas on your ass. Die with honor for your people. Overcome your fears of death because we're already dead men walkin . . . Two, know your area and plan your escape route in advance. If you know where you're going you'll be less hesitant. Getting out of the area as quickly as possible is key and detrimental to your survival . . . Three, leave no evidence. No DNA no nothing. Get rid of anything that can tie you to the area . . . Four, no phones or electronics. Never carry any of that shit with you because they got too many ways to track devices. As a matter of fact, wherever we meet before you set out turn your phones off. I don't want nobody to ever bring their phone in my house again. Leave 'em in your cars and make sure that they're always turned off . . . Five, when you're about to go on that mission alter your description. I want everybody to practice at being a master of disguises. The pandemic allows everybody to wear a mask without drawing attention, take advantage of that opportunity. Wear make-up. Wear wigs, wear clothes you wouldn't be found dead in. Do whatever you got to do to look like someone other than yourself. And once your disguise has served its purpose make that disguise disappear.

For example, you know what I did with the shit I wore that night when I popped those cops?"

"What?"

"I clipped everything up with a pair of scissors and flushed it down the toilet," George said.

"I like that," Fred said.

"Me too."

"After you fire that gun and you do what you do, drop that shit in the lake as soon as you get the chance. You can't afford to get caught with it. If you can't drop it in the lake toss it. And make sure you wipe your fingerprints off of it. As a matter of fact wear gloves. Once you make it to safety wash your hands in a solution. Some bleach or some other type of disinfectant. Don't take any chances. Prepare for everything.

"How long you plan on doing this?" Breonna asked.

"As long as it takes . . . How long have they been killing our people? Like I told y'all before, we didn't choose this path. They chose it for us. This is a very wicked race of people we're dealing with. Don't get me wrong, all white people don't hate us or want to harm us, but at the same time there's millions of them that do. These are the ones that I'm worried about. The criminal justice system is the reorganization of the enslavement of our forefathers. They will always be our enemy. Cops, judges, DA's, prison guards, jailers are the arch enemy of the black communities. We now outnumber whites nine to one in America's prison system. Do you think that that's by accident? The war on drugs that started fifty years ago wasn't actually a war on drugs, it was a war against black and brown communities. Since the war began thousands of black and brown people have been killed, and millions of us have been imprisoned," George said, "Have you noticed that when white people have a problem with drugs they get treatment and counseling? They gave us death and destruction."

"How do you know all this stuff?" Daunte asked.

"I reads, and I reads a lot."

"Why you ain't never shared any of those books with us?" Breonna asked.

"I never thought that y'all would be interested in that kind of stuff, but I was wrong and starting today I'm going to make up for that," George said getting up from the table and heading to his den where he kept a rack filled with all kinds of books concerning black history and the black man's struggle here in America. He returned shortly with a stack of books in his hand.

"You done read all these?"

"Every last one of them," he said as he set the stack of books on the table.

Breonna began reading the title of each book.

"Breaking the Psychological Curse of Willie Lynch . . . The Willie Lynch Papers. . . The Isis Papers. . . Policing the Black Man. . . Before the Mayflower. . . How Europe Undeveloped Africa. . . Message to the Black Man. . . The Destruction of Black Civilization. . . Stolen Legacy. . . Golden Ages of the Moors. . . The Exhuming of a Nation. . . Private Prisons in America . . . The New Jim Crow . . . How to Hustle and Win."

"I want y'all to grab two books apiece and read 'em. Don't be bullshittin either. Make sure you read them. I want you all to have a clear understanding of why and what we're fighting against to increase your courage."

They all picked two books apiece.

"Ahmaud you got some weed?"

"Keeps it," he said pulling a huge sack out of his pocket.

"Gone roll up some blunts and relax. I want y'all to start reading now so we'll all be on the same page. And one state of mine," George said.

Breonna looked at George with such adoration in her heart, it was then that she knew that she had fallen madly in love with him. She wanted him badly now. She began to shake her leg under the table. Her pussy had gotten wet. That sticky moisture was literally boiling between thighs. She squeezed her legs tightly shut as she thought about what she wanted him to do to her.

"Yo man, this some powerful shit. I've only read a couple chapters and I'm already open. All this shit been going on all this time, I can't believe I didn't know nothing about it," Andrew said. He was reading the book called "Policing the Black Man."

"No doubt. This how to hustle and win off the chain. This brother really giving it up."

They all began to comment on the books they were reading, and George could see that it was having a positive effect.

"This New Jim Crow is so deep I don't want to put it down. The way all these white companies been investing in prisons and keeping our communities poor, so we'll go out and commit crimes is unbelievable. These white folks be planning for us to be imprisoned before we're even born. That's some fucked up shit you feel me?" Breonna said shaking her head disappointedly.

"They been systematically oppressing us for a long time. They haven't taken their foot off of our necks since slavery began. They made us hate and kill each other. They trained us to do that. That's why we are the way we are today. This shit is crazy man," Ahmaud said. He was reading "Breaking the Psychological Curse of Willie Lynch."

"How come we don't learn none of this shit in school?" Daunte asked.

"Because instead of doing it ourselves we trust the white man and the white woman to teach our children. You think they're going to tell the truth about what they did to us? Don't get your hopes up. These muthahfuckahs been lying to us for centuries. What made you think that they've changed? Their plan was to enslave us forever. Mentally, spiritually and physically," George said.

"There's a great disturbance in the force," Trayvon said.

"You better believe it. If these muthahfuckahs thought that they was gonah just kill us and oppress us forever, they got another thang coming."

"I know that's right."

"Word up."

"So I guess we supposed to be domestic terrorist now huh?" Breonna said.

"Terrorist! How the fuck is we the terrorist?! When these muthahfuckahs the ones that been raping, kidnapping and murdering us for centuries? The same muthahfuckahs that enslaved us and molested our women and children for hundreds of years. Brutalized and lynched our men. You tell me, who's the terrorist. . . Ah muthahfuckah don't become a terrorist until they start fighting back, you feel me? As long as you accept oppression you good. But as soon as you stand up against injustice you ah terrorist. You woke. You promoting cancel culture, you're a socialist, you're a leftist. I'll be all that. But if ah muthah think they bout to keep killing my people in the street and riding around like something sweet, they might as well get ready to go to Zahmoondah because I promise you that before I die I'm gonah see how many pigs I can give some wings you feel me?"

"No doubt."

"You better believe it."

"Real talk."

"Preach."

We were very much all in agreement. No one could dispute a single word that he had said.

"Let me ask y'all a question," George said as he walked back and forth around the room. "What makes a terrorist a terrorist? . . . When ah muthahfuckah drops a bomb on the man next door and kills him his wife and his kids and they claim they did it because he was a terrorist that's okay isn't it? But in the same process that bomb that was dropped kills everybody in all the next five houses of people that didn't have shit to do with nothing that's supposed to be acceptable too right? . . . But now that those relatives of the people you killed want to retaliate against you for killing their families suddenly they're labeled as terrorist. You feel me? That's how these muthahfuckahs operate. So in all actuality what you have is the real terrorist calling everybody else a terrorist."

"You right. That's damn sure what they be doing."

"I know. And that's why we're taking this stand. A statement has to be made. The only thing the white man respects is violence, and he loves dishing it out. They can kill us all day long then guess what they say?"

"What?"

"March peacefully. I'm tired of marching peacefully. It gottah be consequences. I want these muthahfuckahs to know and understand that when they unjustly kill us or oppress us that somebody in there organization is going to get their wig pushed back."

"They say you reap what you sow," Fred said.

"Real niggahs do real things," Daunte said.

"And what's ah niggah? Ah figure of speech crackers used, they should of looked in a mirror, cause how the fuck could I ever be inferior," Trayvon said.

CHAPTER 8

KILLER BEE

Chief Clinton Sumner was stressed. He was on the verge of losing his job. He was drinking more and more every day. It seemed like nothing would go right for him. No arrest had been made in the killing of the two officers four months ago and the city mayor and the commissioner had been giving him a hard time every day since. And once they announced that the police involved in the killing of Michael Brown would not be charged shit really hit the fan. There had been protests in front of City Hall every day. The community was shocked that the officers had not been charged with murder. Many buildings across the city had been set on fire that day and rioting and looting had devastated the city's business district. Crabtree Valley Mall look like a huge mound of black ashes after hundreds of protesters ransacked the building, looted all the stores and set it ablaze. That mall had stood for decades and now it was all gone. He couldn't remember a time when his job was so hard. For the past few months he'd been thinking more and more about retirement. Just grab the family and get the fuck out of Rocky Mount. Take a long vacation somewhere where the muthahfuckahs don't even speak

English. Anywhere but here he thought. He was in very deep thought when he climbed behind the wheel of his car preparing to make that trip to a work environment that was becoming less and less appealing every day.

As soon as he pulled his door shut something smashed through his back window. "What the?," he ducked his head down because he thought that someone was shooting at him. Then he heard the heavy object roll off of his back seat and hit the car floor with a thud. Somebody flew by on a moped and turned the corner real fast.

"Son of ah bitch! Threw a rock through my window. . . .I'm ah kill this muthahf -."

Chief Sumner's car suddenly exploded. He was blown to pieces. The object that he thought was a rock was actually a hand grenade. Most of his body was instantly incinerated. Chief Sumner's head blew out the front windshield of his car and ended up in a nearby tree. His face was still twisted in that mask of hatred where he was trying to say his last words, "Muthahfuckah!"

Breonna, dressed like a clown, was pushing her little moped as fast as it would go. She was scared shitless. She ran a red light and nearly got crushed by an oncoming Mack truck. The driver of the truck leaned on his horn. Breonna kept going. She didn't look back. She kept it moving. Gold Rock was such a small town that she was out of the city limits within minutes. She turned onto a country back road and drove down the road about a quarter of a mile. A black SUV was pulled off onto the shoulder of the road. She pulled the moped up beside it. George got out, grabbed the moped and flung it into a creek while Breonna climbed into the SUV. Immediately be she began taking off her costume while she hunched down in the back seat of the SUV. George jumped back behind the wheel, and they were gone. He got back on the Interstate and stopped at the first rest stop. Breonna, carrying a bag containing the disguise she wore, went into the ladies restroom. She sat down on the toilet with a pair of scissors, cutting up the clown clothes into little pieces and flushing them down the toilet.

Placing the bag in the trash she walked out of the restroom and got back in the SUV.

"How'd it go?" George asked.

"I think Rocky Mount is going to be needing another police chief," she smiled.

He kissed her, she kissed him back. The kiss got deeper and deeper and more demanding. George felt his dick getting hard. He pulled back breaking the kiss. Breonna moaned in protest. She wanted some more. George put the SUV in drive, and they were back on the road again. They drove down to Virginia Beach where it was already decided that they would spend the next two days. She was so nervous and excited. She could feel the butterflies flapping around in her belly.

"Are you alright?" George asked lightly touching her face with his fingertips.

"I'm terrified . . . I got chills and everything., I just need to get somewhere where you can hold me."

"Trust me I know the feeling."

"I bet you do," she said reaching for his hand. Once they made it to the beach they found a room where they could see the water from their window. It was a breathtaking view. It was really romantic, but Breonna had other things on her mind.

"Come over here and put that big dick in my mouth," she said in a voice which sounded so sweet, "you got some business to take care of."

"You know how to get ah niggah excited don't cha," he said. As he walked towards her while unfastening his pants. She was sitting on the edge of the bed watching, waiting impatiently.

He stood in front of her. Dick hard as hell.

"Damn, this thang long," she said sticking out her tongue and running it over the tip of his dick. She licked on it, slow and tenderly. She didn't use her hands at all. Only her mouth. She played with the head between her lips. Kissing and licking on it like it was her favorite lollypop. She ran her tongue under the bottom of his pole. She let the dick rub against her cheek. A tremor went through his body. She felt it. She smiled as she continued to work on him, licking and kissing her way slowly down the long shaft. She finally reached his heavy nut sack. She opened her little mouth wide and took one of his nuts in her mouth. George groaned in the back of his throat as he swayed a bit. She worked on one nut sucking greedily before moving to the other and repeating the process. She made loud poppin sounds with her mouth as she continued to pleasure him. Still kissing, sucking and licking, she slowly worked her way back up the length of his dick. Once she reached the tip she slowly began taking him into her mouth. Back and forth, back and forth. She took as much of the dick as she could into her mouth.

"Iiiaaaaaugh!," George moaned as he watched his dick disappear into her face. No woman had even done him like this before. He was gone.

Gripping him by his butt cheeks with both of her hands, Breonna began pulling him deeper into her mouth. She made a choking sound several times as several inches of his dick stabbed repeatedly into her throat. She was trying her best to deep throat the thang, but it was just too much. After one more final suck she backed up off of it. She smiled. George was standing there, legs damn near bout to buckle. He was dunk on lust. Aggressively he began snatching off her clothes. Her shirt. Her bra. Her pants. She rolled over onto her stomach and began to crawl away. He snatched her back towards him by her ankles and jerked her panties down, ripping them in the process. Ass went everywhere. Breonna's ass was so big, juicy and soft that when he touched it, it looked like it was melting in his hands. Climbing onto the bed behind her he grabbed her by her large hips and jacked her ass high into the air, immediately he plunged forward.

"Iaaaaaahi! . . . Stooooop," she cried when she felt that long dick slam into her. She tried to run from the dick, but he held her so firmly. Her ass was jacked up so far in the air that her knees were barely touching the bed.

"Unaaah! . . . Unaaah! . . . Unaaah," she moaned as he continued to pull her back against his beastly thrusts.

She wanted him to beat that pussy good, and damn if her wish wasn't coming true. It wasn't her fault that she was crying about it.

"Uaaaaaugh! . . . Wait baby! . . . . Pleeease . . . Oooooh! . . . Oooooh!," she cried as George continued to beat her back out. He looked down at all that ass he was in, and he thought he had done died and went to heaven. The ass was so luscious and fat it looked like it was drippin all over his dick. Breonna put both of her hands behind her in an effort to try to lighten his assault on the pussy. It didn't work much.

"Ooooh! . . . Ooooh! . . . Ooooh baby! . . . Fuck me good . . . Fuck me good! . . . Iaaaaaaiiii! Stoooop!," she cried. She was cummin again.

In one fluid motion George roughly flipped her over, grabbed her tiny little feet and pushed her feet back to her ears. He was already back in the pussy. Rotating his hips like he was at the stove stirring up something gooey. He was tip drilling her. Moving his hips in a circular motion with about two or three inches of the dick in her. She liked that. She started having another orgasm. Standing up on his tip toes in a position like he was about to do some push-ups, George plunged that long dick into her. She screamed, "Iaaaaaiiiiah! . . . Please don't go so deeeeep," she cried. He exploded.

George was twitching and jerking like somebody had hit 'em with a taser. Breonna raked her nails across his back and his buttocks. For several minutes he just laid there between her legs, sweating and breathing heavily with her tiny feet resting on his shoulders.

"That was round one. . . We gonah order some food, smoke a few blunts, then get into round two you feel me? I'm ah tare that pussy up today," he said.

"This your pussy. Look -," she was standing at the window looking out over the water, she bent over and shook that ass at him.

He started getting hard again.

CHAPTER 9

BEHIND CLOSED DOORS

Breaking News . . . . .
"Chief Clinton Sumner of the Rocky Mount Police Department was killed yesterday in what police say was an apparent grenade attack shortly after leaving his house while sitting in his car in his driveway. Police believe that Chief Sumner was preparing for work when he was attacked by an unknown assailant who they've not been able to identify. So far no arrests have been made concerning the incident.

"Witnesses report seeing a person dressed as a clown, riding a moped in the area at the time of the horrific crime. Police are looking for this individual as a person of interest in connection to the incident. As of today Federal Authorities and other agencies have dedicated their support to the Rocky Mount Police Department, and the community, and have pledged resources to assist in bringing those responsible to justice. North Carolina Governor Roger Cooper denounced the act and called it a despicable crime that deserves the harshest punishment under the law. Governor Cooper expressed his sympathy and support for Chief Sumner's family and vowed to use every available asset to make sure that justice would be served.

"So far a massive investigation is being conducted. This tragic moment comes on the heels of the two Rocky Mount police officers that were killed in the parking lot of a Dunkin' Donuts nearly five months ago. Police still have not located the suspect in that case. Police have asked that all officers be vigilant and alert while law enforcement agencies work diligently to solve these senseless acts of crime.

"Anyone with any information in regard to these incidents are asked to call Crime Stoppers or contact the Rocky Mount Police Department. Please be advised that Crime Stoppers does offer cash rewards for any information that leads to an arrest and conviction. For more information you can go to our website at - .
. . . .

"Somebody's out there picking our men off," Commissioner Brinkley of the Rocky Mount Police Department said.

"I agree. It certainly looks like we may have a cop killer on our hands," Heith Werner said, the city's mayor.

"Looks like! I'd say that's an understatement. Three law enforcement officers have been killed and they barely found enough of the last one for his family to bury. It don't look like they're dead to me; they are dead," City Council Manager Nill Falk said. He looked disgusted.

"Who do you think it is? And why?" the mayor asked.

"Isn't it obvious? Officers just killed a man on national TV and nobody's punished for it, don't you think that'll make someone mad enough to try and retaliate. Look what's going on. Police killing's are up around the country and nobody's going to prison for it. The shit is causing riots and all kinds of crap." The commissioner said.

"It's probably those niggers from Black Lives Matter. They're nothing but a bunch of domestic terrorists anyway. Those people don't got no respect for law enforcement and I'm sick of it."

"We gottah do something about 'em."

"Like what?" the mayor asked crossing his legs and folding his hands on the table.

"The commissioner leaned back and put his hands behind his head and interlocked his fingers. City Counselman Falk formed a pyramid with his hands.

"We need stricter penalties and harsher prison sentences for those who violate the law at these rallies," the commissioner said.

"These miserable black bastards are getting out of control, and they need to be put back in their place. They act like they've forgotten who runs this country."

"I agree."

"What are you suggesting Counsel?"

"Stiffer laws and longer prison terms. . . . If a protester blocks traffic, ten years in prison. If a protester throws something at an officer during one of these rallies and injures an officer, five years in prison. If protesters are ordered to disperse and they fail to comply, three years in jail. These people have to be taught a lesson."

"I got one for you."

"Let's hear it."

"If someone runs over a protester with their vehicle while fleeing a protest or because the protester was blocking traffic, that person will not be charged with a crime."

"I like that one."

"Me too."

"I'm going to contract our friends at the General Assembly's Office and ask them to get these laws on the ballot and passed as soon as possible," the mayor said.

"You already know that the democrats are not going to agree to this."

"Who gives a fuck what those socialist, nigger loving bastards think! The republicans control this state. We can pass any laws we want to."

"The Mayor does have a point Counsel."

"I'm just saying we don't need no bad publicity right now. The primaries are coming up in less than a year and –"

"What we don't need is a bunch of niggers running around killing cops and taring up the country," the commissioner said obviously frustrated with the council's lack of steadfastness.

"You're right, I apologize."

"So gentlemen, are we in agreement?"

Both men nodded.

"Very well then, I'll make the necessary calls to get the ball rolling. In the meantime I want you gentlemen to use your connections to increase our support."

CHAPTER 10

TALK OF THE TOWN

Y'all hear about what happened to the top cop?"

"You talking about Sumner?"

"The one and only."

"Hell yeah, I seen that shit on the news . . . somebody turned that niggah into ah milkshake."

"Word up."

"Fuck that house niggah muthahfuckah. He was a enemy to his own people any damn way."

"I'm glad somebody killing they ass, they damn sure been killing us."

"Word."

"Real talk."

"I wonder who it is."

"Who gives ah fuck. Anybody ridin on the oppressor is a friend of mines."

"Mines too."

"I damn sure don't got no love for 'em."

"Me neither."

"All they do is kill niggahs and lock niggahs up, that's it. All dem son of a bitches can suck my dick. You feel me?"

"Word."

A group of young black men were standing around on the corner of Medal Brook, a hot street known for a lot of drug trafficking. Everybody was chilling, just kicking the bullshit and trying to holler at the honeys when they walked by.

The recent cop killing had the communities talking again. There was a lot of speculation, but nobody really knew what was up. But the way it looked; somebody was fighting back. Blacks in the communities that were familiar with the subject were not mad at all. Secretly and openly some even cheered whoever was responsible. Not too many people in the hood were fond of the police. They were the enemy. An evil oppressor which was the offspring of lynch mobs and slave patrollers.

The truth was finally coming out about the system. And white people and their house niggahs were having a fit. White supremacy was under attack definitely. For five months straight there have been marches and rallies going on all over the United States. I'm talking about literally every single day. The people wasn't letting up. For far too long the white men had his knee on the back black man's neck and the people were fed up.

A report about slavery written by a black woman named Nicole Hannah Jones called "The 1619 Project," rocked American society. Her reporting earned her a Pulitzer Prize and a MacArthur genius grant. And it also earned her a racist backlash never seen before by conservatives. The 1619 Project commemorated the arrival of the first enslaved Africans and highlighted the role that slavery played in America's past. The Project showed how out of slavery – and the anti-black racism it required – grew nearly everything that has truly made America great.

Racist senators all over the country vowed to defund K through 12 schools that taught the 1619 Project. They claimed the 1619 Project is a racially divisive and revisionist account of history that threatens the integrity of the Union by denying the true principles on which it was founded.

Conservatives went on the offense and began passing all types of crazy laws to try to stop the 1619 Project from being taught in America. They were mad because African Americans were refusing to allow the white man to lie and teach his own accounts of their history.

It was about damn time.

The more republican lawmakers tried to write the 1619 Project off as just Critical Race Theory, the more publicity it received. Pretty soon more and more people wanted to know what the hell they were so desperately trying to hide.

The truth was being told.

And people were starting to listen.

CHAPTER 11

SHOTS FIRED

Let me tell y'all a little secret that's been kept about prisons for a long time, so you'll have a more clearer understanding of what's been going on and why things are the way they are. It's important that you listen closely.

First of all imprisonment is the aggressive separation of men from women. This is called sexual oppression. Sexual oppression causes perversity. It's like taking an animal out of its natural habitat. Even though you may have taken that animal out of its natural environment, that animal is still going to seek other ways to express its aggressive nature, just like a man that has been separated from a woman, that man that you separated from that woman is going to seek other men or fantasy to express his sexuality.

In an all-male prison this form of oppression will produce homosexuals, child molesters, rapists, and perverts, and bisexuals.

In an all-woman prison this wicked set of human aggression, which they call punishment, will produce lesbians, child molesters, rapists, bisexuals and perverts.

Without a doubt, America's criminal justice system is responsible for creating today's LGBTQ communities, which has also created today's transgender society. I don't tell you these things because I am against the LGBT community. Your all our brothers and sisters and we love you all. I tell you these things to expose those evil men and women who created this system. If you've noticed the conservatives have come out like they're the number one haters against LGBTQI but at the same time these are the muthahfuckahs investing billions in prisons that's responsible for transforming the sexualities of men and women.

They say that this form of punishment is used because it creates weaker men and women because weaker men and women are easier to control. Ain't that some shit?

These muthahfuckah done fucked up that natural order of things now they pretend like it's societies fault. That's what you call a hypocrite of the worst kind.

It's time for revolution!," One of the speakers at the Black Lives Matter rally being held in front of the Governor's Mansion in Raleigh, North Carolina said. There were thousands of protesters gathered in the streets and on the lawn of the Governor's Mansion, protesting against the decades of police brutality and the recent killing of yet another unarmed black man.

A twelve-year-old black boy was playing on the playground with a BB gun when an anonymous person called police to report a black man was on the playground waving a gun. Within 4 seconds of arriving on the scene police shot and killed the little boy.

District Attorney for the county, John Fenner, declined to charge the officers involved, and declared the shooting a justified homicide.

"How much longer America? How many more lynchins will it take for you to quench your thirst on the blood of our men, women and children? It's been over four-hundred years and your evil tactics of invoking hate and fear still persist. This is not the home of the free and the land of the braves. It's the home of the racist and the land of the slaves. Even since the white man stepped on our shores the world have seen nothing but abundant death and destruction. How much longer America? . . . . . A little over four-hundred years ago our people were in bondage and chains. A little over four-hundred years later it's called mass incarceration. Were we ever truly freed? And if so, freed to do what? Free to live under the same laws of oppression of those who raped, kidnapped and murdered us for centuries? Free to obey the laws of those who raped our women and molested our children every day for hundreds of years? That's not true freedom, that's a perpetuation of torment and death!

It's time for change now! I just want to –"

There was a commotion among the police suddenly as they began drawing their weapons and pointing them at the crowd of protesters.

At first no one could figure out what was going on until a huge portion of a policeman's scalp exploded. Blood sprayed like a dust cloud. It was the third officer shot. Then another one got hit in the throat. He dropped to his knees clutching his neck where his esophagus used to be. The police began to scramble and take cover. They still were unable to tell where the shots were coming from. People in the crowd began to run. Lots of screaming and shouts could be heard. The situation quickly turned into chaos as several more officers were shot.

"Sniper! Sniper! . . . get down!," an officer screamed into his walkie-talkie as bodies continued to fall.

"Get down! Get down!"

"This is Sergeant Richard Barnes of the Raleigh Police Department. Please be advised there's an active shooter at the Governors' Mansion. There's been multiple casualties. We need a swat team immediately! Send medical assistance. The shooter is -!" a bullet slammed into his head above his right eye knocking out the majority of his brain which burst out the back of his skull.

"Sergeant Barnes are you there? . . . Sergeant Barnes?"

Sergeant Barnes laid against his squad car with the walkie-talkie still clutched desperately in his hand.

Daunte dropped the 50 caliber assault rifle and ran. Getting from the top of the building to the street was now the main priority. And he knew that he had to move fast. He didn't know how long it would take for them to figure out where the shots came from, but he knew it wouldn't be long.

He was dressed like a woman. Long eyelashes, long blonde wig, long nails and plenty of makeup, long pretty dress and the matching M-95 face mask to go with it. Big black purse. He couldn't afford to wait for the elevator to come so he hit the fire stairs leading down the steps two and three at a time. Forty stories was a long way down, but he was going to do it in record time. He kept running like his life depended on it. In all actuality, it did.

A little less than a minute and a half and he'd already covered twenty-two stories. He was coming down those stairs like a wide receiver running a route. Determined. He slipped and fell once and hopped up like a jack-in-the-box, holding up this dress as he continued to run. His eye shadow was smeared like a woman who'd been crying.

Finally he reached the bottom. He opened up the door and walked across the lobby casually shaking his hips. Nobody seemed aware of what had just happened a little over a mile away.

Daunte stepped out onto the street clutching his purse. He waved down a taxi.

"Where to?," the cab driver asked, as Daunte climbed in.

"Bus station please," Daunte said in his sweetest voice.

The cab driver looked in the rearview mirror at Daunte. He rolled his eyes. "Fuckin fagots," he said to himself.

Dante batted his eyes at the cab driver. The cab drivers' forehead wrinkled. He was obviously frowning underneath his mask.

Less than ten minutes later the cab pulled into the parking lot of the Greyhound Bus station. Daunte's heart was still beating outside his chest. The adrenaline was pumping so hard through his body he thought he was about to faint or have a stroke. Images of him pulling the trigger over and over while the cops scattered in all directions kept popping before his eyes. In all, fourteen cops were dead and twelve were wounded. The mission was a success regardless of whatever happened now.

After paying the cab driver, instead of going straight to the bus station he walked across the street to a gas station and went inside a restroom. Immediately he began taking off the dress and removing the makeup. He didn't have any scissors, so he ripped the dress up with his hands and flushed it down the toilet along with the bra and wig. He rolled his pant legs down that he was wearing under the dress. Pulling out a fitty hat from the purse he placed it on his head and pulled it down tightly over his eyes. Placing a different color M-95 surgical mask on, Daunte stuffed the purse in the restroom trash can. Removed the latex gloves he had on and flushed them down the toilet using the toe of his shoe to press the button. He stepped out of the gas station restroom and walked back across the street to the bus station. He checked the list to see which bus would be leaving the soonest. He found one going to Durham in the next five minutes and he bought a ticket. As he was pulling out of the bus station he saw a convoy of police cars, ambulance and fire trucks approaching.

"This is it," he said to himself.

The convoy of safety vehicles rolled by sirens blaring, lights flashing.

Daunte sat back in his seat and tried to relax. He noticed his hands shaking badly. He crossed his arms and held them tightly against his chest.

The bus pulled out of the bus station, and he was on his way to Durham, North Carolina.

Daunte had a smile on his face.

CHAPTER 12

FRONT PAGE NEWS

"Oh shit!, come check this out, hurry up," Tommy Lee, the owner of the Lee's Bar and Diner said to a passing waitress as he turned up the volume on the big screen TV. "fourteen police officers were killed and twelve were injured when a shooter opened fire from the roof of a nearby apartment building at a Black Lives Matter rally today in Raleigh, North Carolina in front of the Governor's Mansion. Several of the officers are in critical condition, who are now being treated at the Raleigh Memorial Hospital. Police recovered a high powered rifle at the scene, which they believe was used in the shooting. So far there has been no arrests.

"Authorities are looking for this woman who surveillance cameras show leaving the building around the time of the shooting. Law enforcements are on high alert, and they believe that the suspect could still be in the area. Officers have been going door to door at the apartment building asking all residents if they saw or heard anything.

"So far only one witness has come forward. Marico Maddlock, a city cab driver, claims that he drove the suspect to a bus station shortly after the time of the shooting, and that the suspect appeared to be a man dressed as a woman.

"Police are asking the public that if anyone has any information concerning the whereabouts of this suspect or know who this suspect is, please contact the local authorities immediately. Police say the suspect may be armed and is extremely dangerous.

"Police have offered a reward of two-hundred fifty thousand dollars to anyone with any information that leads to an arrest and conviction in regard to this incident.

"A joint effort of law enforcements are currently conducting a nationwide manhunt and have vowed to bring the perpetrator to justice. Many agencies have also dedicated their support and expressed their condolences to the fallen and injured officers, and their families.

"Blue Lives Matter have opened up a GoFundMe account to support all the families of the officers involved in the incident.

"Governor Coopeer has called the crime an act of terrorism and has encouraged law enforcement agencies to work exceptionally hard to bring those responsible to justice. The governor also expressed his support and condolences to all the officers involved in this shooting and their families."

Several protesters recorded the shooting which took place at the rally, and it was now being broadcast all over social media. More than 100 million people saw the video before government officials pressured media outlets to take the sites down. . . . .

Three days later a black man was found with a noose tied around his neck hanging from a telephone pole in Whiteville, North Carolina. Authorities said that it looked like an apparent suicide. Two days later the District Attorney for that county was found hanging from the same telephone pole!

"Yo, Daunte, you all fuckin maniac man. . Goddamn!, you ah fool niggah! . . . Yo, we gottah get this niggah another fifty Cal, word-up. This niggah was on some American Assassins shit you feel me?" Trayvon said, hugging him and patting him on the back.

"No justice. No Peace," Daunte said smiling.

Breonna gave him a kiss on the cheek. Daunte tried to grab a hand full of her ass. She punched him and slapped him upside the head. Daunte grinned.

"Oh my God I can't believe we're really doing this. This the realest shit ever," Fred said.

"Real talk."

"No doubt."

"Real niggah's do real things you feel me."

"While these so called wanta be gangstas out here killing, their own people-n-shit, we gonnah show these muthahfuckahs what time it is, yah heard," Andrew said. Andrew was the one who hung the D.A. on the telephone pole in Whiteville.

"I saw your picture on TV, you was looking real sexy," Ahmaud said, laughing.

"Don't get it twisted muthahfuckah, ain't shit sweet," Daunte said.

"Bee you did a good job on his make-up." George said.

"Could any of y'all tell it was me?," Daunte asked.

"I couldn't."

"Me neither."

"Nope."

"That's good. . . That's all I was worried about, other than that cab driver that tried to rat me out. I was thinking of going back and pushing that clown's wig back you feel me?"

"Chill. Don't even worry about that, we gottah stay focused."

"So what's next?"

"I want'ah pop that D.A. who refused to prosecute those officers in the Michael Brown killing." Eric said.

"That's not a bad idea."

"I'm going with you," Trayvon said.

"This what we gonnah do then. We gonnah chill out for a little while then we gonnah crank it back up, you feel me?"

"That's what's up."

"Yo, where the weed at?," Breonna said.

"I got about a half a pound in the shed," George said.

"Well, it sure ain't doing us no good in the shed. I'm tryin tah get my high on."

"Me too."

"You feel me?"

"Tighten up man."

George took a trip to the shed. He returned a few minutes later. Drinks were already being poured and blunts were being busted open. It was time to relax and unwind. Party a little. Enjoy life as much as possible. Because in their line work nothing was promised.

Definitely not.

CHAPTER 13

STATE SPONSORED

A small group of off duty police officers were gathered together in a large double-wide trailer in a deep wooded area in Halifax County, North Carolina on a cold winter night in November.

Several pickup trucks with AR-15s on gun racks lined the driveway.

A secret meeting was being held where certain issues needed to be discussed concerning the recent spree of cop killings.

Somebody was going to pay.

Police officers from all over the state were at this meeting. There were also several officials from other states. These men represented a secret society within America's law enforcement agencies. A right wing white supremacist group with ties to every state and federal law enforcement agency in the country. An organization which was formed in 1865 by slave patrollers, lynch mobs and the Klu Klux Klan, backed by powerful politicians in the legislature. These men operated at every level of policing. And their mission was the same since its inception; The re-enslavement of blacks and all non-white races by using tactics of mass imprisonment, fear, brutality and murder. These were the good old boys; charged with keeping niggers in their place. The very core of racism itself. They employ millions of members from all walks of life. Judges, lawyers, D.A.s, doctors, movie stars, banking corporations, housing market, sports, entertainment and every major industry in the United States. These men were well connected.

"OK gentlemen, settle down, we're ready to start the meeting," said Sheriff John Brown from Alabama.

Most of the group took their seats but many of them remained standing.

"Gentlemen I received a call from some of our most dedicated friends and they're concerned about the direction our country is heading. They feel that white authority is being challenged and that we need to put a stop to this insurrection immediately."

"I'll tell you how me and my boys are gonnah start, by putting more bullets in niggahs heads."

"Yeah!"

"That's what we're going to do!"

"Goddamn niggers."

A murmur went through the audience of white men gathered inside the trailer as white fists and guns were raised in agreement.

"Calm down my fellow comrades. I totally agree, this conglomerate of left wing socialist must be brought to their knees. We have to teach these Marxists a lesson. The time has come once again where we must strike. And we must act with precision. The current democratic leadership doesn't have the guts to do what's necessary to uphold the values that we hold dear in this country. Therefore someone must step up to the plate and exercise a more heavy-handed approach."

"What's the plan Sheriff?"

"ANTIFA and Black Lives Matter," the Sheriff said.

"Goddamn domestic terrorist!," a member of the group said.

"These two organizations are a threat to our national security, and they must be dealt with by all means accordingly."

"What's the directive?"

Sheriff Brown looked over the room at the dedicated group of men, he knew that all of them would freely give their lives for the cause. He adored them.

"Mass arrest, imprisonment and assassination. A lot of these leaders at these rallies are causing a lot of trouble for our established law and order and we must bring them down before many of them decide to become martyrs. Be vigilant my friends, our cause and mission has more support than you can possibly imagine."

In Elizabeth City, North Carolina one week after the secret meeting of the police officers Andrew Junior, a black man, was fatally shot by sheriff's deputies attempting to serve a search warrant for drug charges. Police in riot gear entered the home of the black man, who was unarmed, and tried to arrest him. For some unknown reason the man ran out his back door, jumped in his car and attempted to flee from the scene. Officers immediately opened fire shooting the black man five times with a fatal shot to the back of the head while he was driving away.

The county District Attorney and the judge overseeing the matter refused to allow the release of the body Cam footage to the public.

Also, it was announced by the district attorney's office that the officers involved in the shooting would not be charged.

After the decision the city manager immediately declared a state of emergency and beefed up their law enforcement presence to counter any protest or riots.

During a traffic stop in Minneapolis an unarmed black man was fatally shot and killed by a white policewoman who repeatedly told the suspect that she was going to tase him before pulling out her service revolver and shooting a black man in the chest.

The investigation is ongoing.

An unarmed black man selling loose cigarettes in front of a convenience store in New York City was killed when a white police officer placed the suspect in a chokehold and suffocated him to death.

No charges were filed against the officers.

In Kentucky police using a no-knock warrant raided the home of a black woman whose residents police believed was being used to traffic drugs. Police fired a barrage of bullets into the woman's bedroom killing her instantly. No charges were filed against the officers involved in the incident.

There were no drugs found.

Many black men, women and children were being killed all over the United States and in 99% of the cases they were being labeled justifiable homicides. These men, women, and children didn't realize that they were being systematically targeted. They had the slightest clue. They were blind to the facts of how racism influences American politics, culture and laws. They were a nation of people who had been miseducated for centuries and taught not to put much consideration into these kinds of issues. They were accustomed to the reality of thinking that if it don't affect me and mines then it's none of my business. They were blind, many of them. They had lost their will to fight back. Millions oppressed to the point of hopelessness hoping and praying that Jesus would hurry up and come back and save them.

The more they marched and protested against police brutality and injustice the more unarmed black men all over the United

States continued to be killed. They were powerless. A people being ruled by those who enslaved them who constantly wondered why there is no justice on their behalf.

Why are we oppressed?

When will it end?

So many unanswered questions for a race of people who'd been beaten down forever it seemed. No justice, no peace, for those who carried the weight of their tormentors burden . . .

But something unexpectedly happened during that time. Not everyone was sleeping.

Some were woke.

Not everyone was in fear. Some were fearless. And as police killings and brutality increased so did their courage.

The desired effect and tactics that were used for centuries by slave masters to break their slaves and keep them in a constant state of fear miraculously backfired.

A new era in time arose.

A statement was made.

"Get your knee off my neck muthahfuckah!"

The tables began to turn.

CHAPTER 14

I DIDN'T SEE NOTHIN

Two Elizabeth City police detectives were sitting in an unmarked police car on Ehringhaus Street, conducting surveillance on a suspected drug dealer for the past hour. Ulysses Edwards, who was also a tattoo artist, sold drugs like most black people do, to support his family and take care of his basic needs. It wasn't like he was part of a cartel pushing tons of coke, but yet and still he always found himself being constantly harassed by the police.

"They out there again," Ulysses said.

"Who?," his girlfriend who was seven months pregnant with their second child asked.

"Them two hateful ass crackers that's always fuckin with me. . . they hate to see a black man trying to survive," he said peeking out the window for the third time. When he first spotted them he immediately went outside into the woods and buried his stash. There's no way he could afford to go to jail. He had a baby on the way. Something like that would destroy his family. He wondered why they wouldn't leave him alone. In all actuality they were just trying to intimidate him. They enjoyed seeing the fear they commanded with their presence. Officer Hightower, one of the detectives, wanted to go knock on the door just to see if the nigger made a funny move, so he'd have ab excuse to shoot him he thought.

From out of nowhere two men appeared on both sides of the car. They were both dressed in suits. One of the men had on a President Donald Trump mask and the other had on a Vice-president Mike Pence mask. They were both wearing black gloves and they both were leveling AR-15s at the faces of the two detectives sitting in the car. Fred tapped on the window with the barrel of the assault rifle.

The officers looked up startled.

"Smile for the camera pigs," he said as he and Ahmaud began simultaneously pulling their triggers.

Right before they pulled the trigger, Ulysses peeked out of his curtain just in time to see the car light up. He couldn't believe what he was witnessing. A total of sixty bullets went into the car. Two thirty-round clips. The two cops looked like they were break dancing as they jerked and twitched every time a slug hit 'em

Closed casket. Somebody called 911.

"What's going on? Who's doing all that shooting out there?" Ulysses girl friend asked.

Ulysses watched the two men that had did the shooting run away.

"I don't know. I didn't see nothing," he said. Ulysses was smiling.

CHAPTER 15

LOYAL TO THE CAUSE

The word was starting to spread, up and down the coast. Somebody was retaliating against cops. The day of reckoning had finally come. Somebody out there was fed up with the bullshit and they were taking matters into their own hands.

Extreme measures.

Centuries of systemic racism, brutality, and oppression had reached a boiling point like no other times before. It was too late to apologize.

How did we get here?

Could these tragic events have been avoided?

Who was responsible?

In a society where those who had sworn to protect us purposely neglected their duty, and instead became the mainspring of the oppression we opposed a tipping point unfolded. Passiveness turn into aggression. Fear turned into rage. And hate was the absence of love that was never there to begin with.

After being asleep for more than four centuries suddenly he'd been shaken from his deep slumber. The Curse of Willie Lynch was crumbling. The system that had been put in place by slave masters so many hundreds of years ago was collapsing on all sides.

A great awakening was in progress.

And the more that ole hateful oppression tried to contain it, the more it burst through the scenes.

Why did they do it?

Who in their right mind builds an empire on hate, discrimination and racism and thinks that it will stand forever?

Fools!

They thought that they would bury the black race for eternity. They believed that they destroyed every ounce of pride and courage they had.

They left us for dead.

Mentally dead.

They cast us off as forgotten.

They called us boy.

They humiliated us for hundreds of years.

We were taught to fear them.

Truly they believed that we would never rise up against them.

They were wrong.

A terrible mistake.

In their attempt to extinguish our fire they overlooked the embers smoldering beneath the pile of ashes.

And it was that little spark of light that eventually turned into a raging inferno.

In the parking lot of a McDonald's in Atlanta, Georgia, Marcus Brooks had fallen asleep at the wheel. He'd been working all day and decided to have a couple of beers then grab a bite to eat before heading home for the night.

As he was waiting in line at the drive-thru he dozed off. One of the restaurant employees called the police because Mr. Brooks' car was blocking traffic.

Knock . . . Knock . . . Knock . . .

"Huh," Mr. Brooks said looking around a little confused and startled.

A police officer was tapping on his glass. "Sir, you need to move your car, you're blocking the drive-thru," the cop said.

"Oh, I'm sorry officer," Brooks said trying to look alert.

When the cop walked away Brooks dozed off again., he didn't realize how tired he really was. He must have had a little too much to drink.

Knock . . . Knock . . . Knock . . .

Brooks suddenly snapped awake again. The same police officer was tapping on his glass again.

"Sir, are you alright? You've fallen asleep again. I told you that you have to move your car," the cop said, looking at Brooks suspiciously.

Brooks smiled and apologized to the officer again. This time he pulled into the parking lot across the street so he could shake the sleep from his eyes and head on home. He was only a few blocks away from his sister's house and thought he'd grab a bite to eat there instead. He was in the process of rubbing his eyes –

Knock . . . Knock . . . Knock . . .

Brooks looked up. It was the same cop again, and he had another cop with him this time. Brooks rolled his window down. He smiled.

"How may I help you officers?" he said.

"We need you to step out of the car sir," the second officer said.

"Why, what's going on?" Brooks asked. A pang of fear stabbed the pit of his stomach.

"Just step out of the fucking car and don't give us a hard time O.K.," the same officer said snatching Brooks car door open.

"What's going on what did I do wrong?"

"We have a warrant for your arrest. Now put your hands on the car where we can see 'em while we search you."

Brooks put his hands on his car. The cop started frisking him. Brooks immediately noticed how ruffly the cop was handling him. He suddenly jerked away from the cops and turned towards them. they grabbed him and forced him to the ground where they began to struggle. Brooks threw both of the officers off of him, grabbed one of their tasers and took off running across the parking lot with the two cops chasing him.

Before Brooks got halfway across the parking lot one of the cops stopped, drew his weapon, and fired three quick shots . . Bang! . . . Bang! . . . Bang! All three shots struck Brooks in the back killing him instantly.

As Brooks' lifeless body lay on the pavement the cop that shot him walked up and kicked him after he was already dead.

"I got 'em!," the cop said as he stood over Brooks' body.

A little black girl named Darnela Davis recorded the entire incident on her phone. She was lucky to be alive because if one of the cop's bullets had missed surely she would have been struck because Brooks was running right towards her.

The video of the cop killing went viral.

One week after the killing of Marcus Brooks by police, Trayvon and Eric hopped on a train and headed to Atlanta. They showed up on the scene looking like they were straight out of Jamaica. Long dreadlocks, thick black shades and green, black and red everything. They were both wearing thick chains made out of wood with different types of African culture on display.

They even spoke like they were Jamaicans. It took them about three and one-half hours to reach their destination.

They didn't speak much at all during the trip. Only enough to leave a good impression, to make people around them believe that they were foreigners.

When the train finally stopped it felt like their hearts did the same thing. The fear was clearly there, but the will and the determination was stronger. The mission was clear, strike back at the enemy. There were no more free passes.

If they were going to continue to kill us because of the color of our skin, then they would also learn that it came with a price. Huge price. A heavy price is what they call it.

After leaving the train station they jumped in an Uber and headed downtown. They directed the cab driver to do a little site seeing. And he was happy to oblige. It was the middle of winter and it had just snowed the day before. The roads were clear but there was plenty of snow still on the ground. Atlanta was a beautiful city by far. Eventually the cab driver took them to a motel where they paid for a room and sat down to discuss their plan. Once they were settled in, Eric unzipped his backpack and pulled out a submachine gun with a one hundred round drum attached to it. He checked the weapon to make sure it was ready. Trayvon did the same.

"O.K., you already know what time it is. We stick to the script. We gottah case the area and figure out at least two to three escape routes before we move, yah dig."

"No doubt. I'm already on top of that and I know just how we gonah do it," Trayvon said, cocking the submachine gun and putting it on fully automatic.

"Do tell," Eric said sitting on the edge of the bed and pulling out a box of blunts and some weed. He rolled two big ass blunts and handed one to Trayvon, who immediately fired up.

He took a deep pull into his lungs and blew out a huge cloud of smoke.

"When we were cruising around Bankhead I noticed some shot spotters."

"You talking bout those gadgets the police be using to track muthahfuckahs when somebody starts shooting?"

"Exactly. That's how we're going to draw them to the scene. When they arrive, we don't play with them or give 'em a chance to breathe. We dumpin the whole fuckin clip and leaving these bitch ass muthahfuckahs slumped, you feel me?"

"Word up."

"Come on it's time to go to Wal-Mart."

"What for?"

"We gonah cop a couple of bicycles and perfect our plans a little more before we ride on these rude boys Star," Trayvon said in his best Jamaican accent.

"Yeah man," Eric replied, with a wicked grin.

It was just starting to get dark when Eric and Trayvon rode their bikes into the hood.

"Are you scared?" Trayvon said.

"Shitless. But it is what it is. If somebody don't take a stand, nobody will. And besides, we're the only ones left that hasn't put in any work for the cause . . . You're not ready to punk out are you?"

"Fuck no! I couldn't live with myself if I did. It ain't about me. This for our people. I'm so tired of watching our women cry because one of these pigs don took away a loved one . . . You just don't know how that shit makes me feel."

"I think I do. And that's why we're here."

They peddled the rest of the way in silence. It was another cold winter night in the city. Cold or no cold the dope heads and the dope pushers were out here. Trap season was an event that lasted all year long. If the money was still being printed, somebody had to go get it.

As they were coasting down the street a very pretty girl with blue hair asked them if they were looking for some pussy. Trayvon threw her the peace sign and kept it moving. The girl rolled her eyes and gave them the bird.

Once they reached the end of the street, it was time for some action.

"Here goes nothing," Trayvon said as he pulled the machine gun from his backpack and sprayed a burst of gun fire into the air. Guah! Guah! Guah! Guah! Guah! Guah! Guah! Guah! The shots sounded like thunder and lightning. Seven and one-half minutes later they were looking down the long road when they spotted the two police cars turn onto the block. They were traveling about five miles per hour as they shined their spotlights from one side of the street to the other.

"They comin," Eric said.

"You ready?," Trayvon asked.

"Got no choice but to be."

They both were wearing heavy jackets with their machine guns tucked up under their arms, with Black Lives Matter stenciled on their surgical masks. They had their bikes leaning against a telephone pole. The two cop cars came to almost a complete stop alongside them.

"You take the first car out, I'll hit the second one up," Trayvon said.

"Bet."

It was show time.

"Hey, is everything alright gentlemen? We heard shots in this area."

"We heard 'em too officer, and it sounded like this -," Eric said as he pulled out the machine gun from underneath his coat and opened fire. Trayvon reacted simultaneously.

"IIIAAAAAAAAAAAAAIIIIah!" Eric screamed as he continued to empty his magazine into the police cars. The first wave of bullets hit the officer in the first car on his cheek bone and knocked his entire jaw off. When the paramedics showed up they found the lower part of the officers jaw sitting on the seat next to him. In the second car at least six bullets hit the officer in the neck and left him looking like he'd just come from up under the guillotine. His head was barely attached to his body. As a matter of fact, when they pulled his body from the car to load him at the coroners, the muthahfuckahs head fell off.

Damn. Them boys done fucked around and faced some shit.

With no hesitation they dropped their weapons and got on that bike.

Time to evacuate.

CHAPTER 16

AFTER THE RALLY

Say, his name!!!"
        "Terrance Franklin!!!!"
        "Say, his, name!!!"
"Terrance Franklin!!!!"
"No justice!!!"
"No peace!!!"
"No justice!!!"
"No peace!!!"
"What do we want?!!!"
"Justice!!!"
"When do we want it?!!!"
"Now!!!"
Thousands of people were gathered together for the March on Washington. There had to be more than seven hundred thousand people there. If this large gathering of protesters decided to act up like those white folks did on January 6th this would have gotten out of hand really quick. This was one of the largest rallies thus far. Some news reporters believe that there had to be more

than a million people in attendance. They say it looked like Dr. King's, 'I Have A Dream' speech.

"Once again we're here, out here in these streets demanding justice from the greatest oppressor we've ever known since we've been on this earth. A relentless and evil being, dedicated to the subjugation and exploitation of all people of color forever.

"In the last forty years a ruthless enemy that climbed to the heights of the world through means of the rape, kidnapped, murder and enslavement of our people. These are men and women that believe in their hearts that slavery would never end for the African and Latino races. And they have worked diligently to establish this status quo.

"They have no dignity. Oppression, discrimination, racism, and hate, are the tools that they use to fuel the success of their worldwide business., of brutality, torture and murder in their designed methods of control.

"How dare they think for another millisecond that we're going to continue to exist like this. Do they not realize that the world has evolved? These muthahfuckahs must think that we're still living in the stone ages. Or that we're still being ruled by cruel kings and Queens.

"No America. I'm sorry, but you seem to be stuck in the wrong time zones.

"The good old days are over.

"And if you really think you're going to continue to treat us as less than human, then you got another thing commin.

"We've beared all that we can bear. We've stood all that we can stand.

"We've endured enough pain and suffering. No more fear.

"If you want peace, we'll be peaceful. But if you cause destruction, may Hellfire rain down from heaven and consume you and every last hateful oppressor," said Rodney King, one of the speakers at the March on Washington Rally.

The crowd erupted in cheers. There was plenty of shouting and fist pumping. People were smiling and clapping their hands as the energy of the political speech spread like wildfire. It seemed like everybody was holding up their phones recording the event.

George, Breonna, Andrew, Fred, Ahmaud and Daunte were among the crowds of people witnessing history.

The speech exhilarated their dedication to the cause even more.

They could relate to the vibe, totally.

Eric and Trayvon decided to lay low for a little while. They were still a little paranoid from their recent experience. The crew understood exactly how they felt. It was an emotion they all dealt with after they killed a cop.

There was no love lost.

It goes with the territory.

The next speaker took the podium. Breonna raised her phone. She was so short she couldn't get a good shot.

"Damn I can't see shit. I wanted to record this for Eric and Trayvon," she said.

George bent down.

"Come on. You can sit on my shoulders," he said.

She smiled, looked at the rest of the crew then climbed on his neck. He lifted her up in the air.

"Can you see now?"

"Perfect," she said smiling raising her phone. George could feel her pussy on the back of his neck burning through her pants. His dick began to rise. He wanted her.

When they got back to North Carolina everybody went their separate ways. George and Breonna decided to explore a little unfinished business. She was sitting on the couch with her tiny feet in Georges' lap. He was rubbing them and holding them in his big hands. He leaned towards her. She leaned towards him. She stuck her little tongue out. He stuck his out. Their tongues touched and a fire began to build inside them. The kisses became more and more intense. More wanting as they sucked on each other's tongues and lips. It sounded like Rice Krispie's popping in your bowl of cereal.

George pulled her onto his lap. He held her close as he continued to invade her mouth with his tongue. She could feel the lump in his pants grinding against her ass.

She reached for it.

She squeezed it.

She stroked it.

She played with it.

She wanted to put her mouth on it.

Suddenly he sat her back down on the couch. Aggressively he began snatching her jeans and panties off. Getting down on his knees he parted her legs and got between them.

A big fat hairy pussy greeted him. The scent of perfume and sweet pussy filled his nostrils. He plunged his long finger inside her pussy hole. She jerked a little. He added another finger to his first one and she began to moan as he dug inside her passage.

Grabbing her legs underneath her thighs she opened her legs even wider as he played in the pussy. She smiled.

He began plunging his fingers in and out of her faster. She moaned.

George leaned forward and opened the pussy wide with both of his thumbs exposing her pink silky folds. He stuck his mouth to her honey box and sucked the pussy real hard.

"Iaaaaugh!" she cried out when he pulled on the sensitive flesh with his lips.

"Iaaaaugh!" she cried out when he did the same thing again.

Still holding the pussy open with his thumbs. George licked the pussy slowly. He covered the whole pussy with his mouth and plunged his tongue as deep as he could inside her. She began to tremble and shake.

George began to move his tongue around inside her.

"Ooooh! . . . yeeeesss, Ooooh!, Ooooh!," she moaned as he repeatedly plunged his tongue inside her stickiness.

Breonna put her little feet on his shoulders and placed her hands on both sided of his head. George sucked the pussy a little bit harder.

"Ooooh! . . . It's cummin!, It's cumin!," she cried as he lapped up every bit of her tangy juices.

Flipping her over and jacking her ass high into the air, George plunged his tongue back inside of her. Breonna grabbed her luscious ass cheeks and pulled them open wide. George started planting wet kisses and hickies all around her pussy. She started cumin again.

As he continued to lick and suck on the pussy slowly and greedily, he began to unfasten his pants.

As soon as she started cumin again he stuck that long black dick in her to the hilt.

"Iaaaaaiii!," she cried out in pleasure and surprise as he split her pussy lips apart.

"Ooooh! . . . Ooooh! . . . Ooooh Yessss!," she cried every time he rammed that meat into her.

"Aaaaugh! . . . Aaaaugh! . . . Aaaaugh!, Oh this pussy good. Oh this pussy so good," he groaned every time he stabbed her with his spear. With one knee on the couch and one foot on the floor he continued to plow into her from behind.

The way her ass jumped and swayed every time he smashed into it only added to his excitement. It was the beginning of a long night of love making.

Flipping her back over George grabbed her tiny little feet and pushed them back damn near to her ears.

He slammed the dick home again.

Breonna screamed.

CHAPTER 17

WHAT HAPPENED?

George woke up the next morning to the sounds of Breonna screaming and shouting. Quickly he jumped up and ran downstairs to see what the commotion was all about. His heart was racing fast. A million thoughts were flashing through his mind as he wondered about the countless possibilities of what could be wrong.

"George hurry up!," Breonna shouted.

When George came into the living room she was jumping up and down pointing at the television.

"Look!" she said.

Scenes of a building with a huge portion of the building destroyed were flashing across the screen as the news reporter described what had happened.

"An unknown black man walked into the Los Angeles Police Department today with a fully automatic weapon and opened fire. The suspect was wearing a bulletproof vest along with several pieces of military style tactical gear when he engaged police in a bizarre gun battle.

"This incident occurred while police were conducting shift change.

"Dozens of officers rushed to the scene to assist in the ensuing battle when suddenly the suspect detonated a bomb which he had strapped to his body. The bomb caused a huge deadly explosion which destroyed a very large portion of the Los Angeles Police Department headquarters.

"So far more than two hundred officers are believed to be dead and hundreds of more injured.

"Officials are calling this the most horrific attack since September the 11th. Right before the attack the suspect posted a video pledging his support for the Black Lives Matter movement and all the families of those whose loved ones that have been killed by police.

"Police have launched an investigation to determine whether or not someone may have assisted the suspect who they have now identified as Michael Johnson.

"Please stay tuned. More details coming up next."

"We love you Michael Johnson!," Breonna screamed.

George had a look on his face of total respect. As Breonna hugged and kissed him.

"That's what you call a real trooper."

"Yup."

"That dude wasn't playing no games. . . .God damn MJ."

"We need a whole lot more like him," Breonna said.

"Don't worry, they're coming. These muthahfuckahs are so drunk off of oppressing us for centuries that they don't even realize that their calling them out," George said.

"It ain't my fault. Did I do dat? It ain't my fault. Did I do that?," Breonna started singing the lyrics to one of her favorite rap songs. She smiled.

"That niggah was the real Magic Johnson and I apologize for using the n-word. Goddamn!" George said still shaking his head. He was standing in front of the TV in his boxers. Breonna was sitting on the floor beside him. She turned towards him and quickly plunged her little hand into his boxers.

As soon as she grabbed ahold of his member it began to rise in her hand. She looked up into his eyes. He looked down into hers.

She smiled.

He smiled.

She yanked the dick out of his boxers and began plunging it in and out of her mouth repeatedly.

Good Morning America.

CHAPTER 18

THE NEW WAR

W ho the fuck is this niggah Michael Johnson? I want to know everything about him. I want to know who his family is. His friends. Any girlfriends. His dogs name and anywhere he might of took a shit in the last 10 years . . . I want answers goddamnit!" Federal Field Commander Chip Mitchell said, banging his fist on his desk. The office was filled with counterterrorism officers assigned to investigating the Los Angeles Police Department bombing attack.

"The Army has over 450 separate record centers containing substantial information on civilian political activities. Virtually every major Army unit has its own set aside for this," said Special Agent John Stokes.

"By Mr. Johnson being ex-military we're going to dig into his background there also. There's been a forty percent increase in police killings within the last two years. We gonah check out all the people who were in Mr. Johnson's unit and try to figure out if a team might be operating."

"It's possible, due to the fact that these police attacks are occurring all over the country," Mitchell said.

"Has there ever been a spike like this?," Stokes asked.

"Never. I've never seen nothing like this in all the thirty years I've been in law enforcement," Mitchell said.

"Me neither," another agent said.

"What do you think's causing it?"

"That's a obvious question . . . come on, . . . you're an intelligent officer aren't you? . . . Police keep killing these niggahs and nobody's going to jail for it. What do you think they're going to do?"

"It may be time to end the war on drugs and prepare for a new one," Mitchell said.

"I agree."

"I believe what we're seeing here is the tip of the iceberg."

"If niggahs all over the country start participating we could have a National Security situation on our hands."

"It looks like we're already heading in that direction."

"How do we stop it?"

"I'd say the same way we stopped the Black Panther Party, if you asked me."

"I think those methods are a little outdated don't you think?"

"No."

"This ain't the 60's and 70's, these black uprisings have changed."

"Fuckin Black Lives Matter movement."

"The Black Panther Party didn't have half these many followers."

"There's a Black Lives Matter chapter in damn near every state. If we start knocking off their leaders we'll need a lot more than the National Guard to contain them," Mitchell said.

"We have a lot more than the National Guard."

"Say goodbye to democracy."

"Democracy is already dead. Since Joe Biden took office this country has turned into a socialist nightmare," Stokes said.

"Goddamn niggah loving Marxist."

"We might be at the point of no return."

"These niggahs are not that smart."

"Try telling that to the Los Angeles Police Department."

"The FBI has organized an impressive armament of resources and equipment. We try to monitor situations and get to them before they become emergencies. No expense will be spared in this new monitoring program. Yeah we're going to enforce a massive surveillance operation targeting this radical black lives matter movement and we're going to do everything in our power to crush this domestic terrorist organization," Mitchell said. "we're going to use every possible method at our disposal to destroy them."

Law enforcement agencies all over the United states were highly concerned after seeing what happened in Los Angeles. New tactics were being implicated on a daily basis. Throughout history small but powerful groups of people have constantly felt that they alone had the power to control the public races. And for centuries this has proven to be true. But something must have gone wrong. This system of control was starting to malfunction at a crippling rate. A rebellion had started, and it was spreading fast.

A sense of fear and uncertainty began to set in for police as more and more cops were killed.

Should anyone of a liberal mind say that such reflections as these are immoral? If it is possible for any logical mind to wish with any success to guide crowds of people by the aid of reasonable counsel and agreements when any objection or contradiction, senseless as it may be, can be made and when such objections may find more favor with the people whose powers of reasoning and agreement are superficial, then who is to blame when the people stand against tyranny.

In any state in which there are bad organizations of authority, and impersonality of law, and of its rulers who have lost their personality amid a tide of rights ever multiplying, a new right will be founded to attacks by the right of the oppressed and to scatter to the winds all existing forces of order and regulations that exist in a system of perpetual mentally and physical slavery.

The abstraction of freedoms due to centuries of bondage demands accountability.

If none of the above is true, something else must be happening which is beyond our ability to understand or control.

Through ignorance or misplaced trust we as a people have abdicated our role as the watchdog over our government. A government was founded of the people, for the people, by the people.

White people.

Blacks were forced to abdicate their role and their place in the world and put total trust in a small group of white men who meet secretly to decide their fates. Evil men who hated them because of the color of their skin. Believing all the while that these facts could not possibly be true blacks fell asleep hoping, wishing and praying for the American dream. Which always continued to delude them.

The capacity for the abuse of power against blacks dated all the way back to 1619. The continuation of that process was being questioned.

CHAPTER 19

TRAGIC EVENTS

Y ou got the whole fuckin world talkin about Michael Johnson."

"I bet you do. The niggah look like he came straight
out of ah fuckin Rambo movie, ah fool!"

"Word-up."

"I'm talkin about your boy went ham. . . he blew the whole
Goddamn police department off the map. He's ah animal," Trayvon said.

"And we thought we was making a statement," Fred said.

"You feel me? . . . That shit look like a fuckin nuclear bomb
went off in that muthahfuckah. . . That's some real live Mad Max
shit, yah-heard?," Eric said.

"Real talk, they still pulling bodies from the rubble," George
said.

"I don't feel not one drop of remorse for them hateful bastards. Do you realize how many black people the Los Angeles
Police have killed? You wouldn't believe it."

"All that military shit they got didn't do em no good that time
did it?"

"Hell, naw! They fucked around and got caught sleepin. Thinking shit was gonnah be sweet forever."

"I know that's right," Breonna said.

"They say that niggah had ten sticks of dinomite with a bunch of C-4 wrapped around that shit," Daunte said.

"These crackers don turned us into a bunch of maniacs in this bitch."

"That's what they wanted, ain't it?," Andrew said.

"No doubt."

"I'm talking bout, look what the fuck they keep doing to us. How the fuck you gonnah feel if muthahfuckahs say some shit like. 'We killed your dad by accident, I thought I was reaching for my taser,' . . . Hell naw bitch! . . 'Oh, we thought he had a gun, but it was his cell phone,' . . . Fuck that shit! So you mean to tell me that they don made this mistake thousands of times and we suppose to be good with dat? . . . Hell naw! Muthahfuckahs. We gon get it back in blood," Ahmaud said.

The atmosphere in the room was hyped-up. Drinks were being poured. Blunts were being passed.

The reality of how their lives just suddenly changed was almost hard to believe. They went from being normal people to being cop killers damn near over-night. The things that were happening in society could be felt like a stab to the heart with a very long knife. It was shocking, and impossible to ignore.

Being black and oppressed in America was real, and it wasn't something that had just started. These industries were a continuation from the past. Slavery. For a long time people were made to believe that things had gotten better, then in all actuality, they remain the same. Men, women and children were still being chained and put in cages. Men, women and children were still being brutalized. Men, women and children were still being lynched. One must wonder, . . . "What was Emancipation?"

"So what we doing next?" Andrew asked.

"We chillin . . . When they act up we act up, you feel me. If they kill our people we kill theirs, straight like that," George said.

"WE NEED SOME MORE GUNS,"

"I wish I can get my hands on ah fuckin bazooka."

"Word up."

"Hollar at our Mexican and see what's up. Let 'em know we trinah cop something big," George said.

"Yo, while we're chillin we need to cop some more work and run our bread bad up, you feel me? We gottah be on deck when it's time to make a move so we won't be scrambling around like we was when we first started."

"No doubt."

"Yo, y'all see if y'all can get another spot jumpin. . . We got a little over two hundred and fifty thousand left in the stash. We gonnah spend a hundred on guns and a hundred on dope. . . we gonnah split the rest and ball 'til we fall, you feel me?"

"I like the sound of that. If I'm gonnah live life on the edge I'd rather do it in a fresh pair of new Jordans." Daunte said.

"Jays on my feet, Jays on my feet."

"Fuck Jordan, that niggah support prisons!"

"Say word!"

"That's what I heard."

"I heard the same thing."

"Well fuck what yah heard, I'm still getting me at least two more pair before we boycott you feel me?" Daunte said smiling.

"Oh Lord," Breonna said rolling her eyes.

George came in the room and a placed two bags on the table. He turned it over and dumped out the contents. bundles of fifties and hundred dollar bills were sitting in a pile in the middle of the table. After setting the two-hundred thousand to the side – "There's fifty-three thousand, eight hundred dollars left for us to split. Take it and enjoy yourselves," George said.

"That's what's up," Trayvon said.

"We should have the spot up and jumpin in a few days," Eric said.

"That's good. The sooner the better," George said.

"Make sure you ask about that bazooka, you heard," Ahmaud said grinning wickedly.

"Will do."

Within no time the trap house was up and running and the dough was piling up again. Everybody was doing their part. The gun deal was a success except for the bazooka. The Mexican wanted twenty-five thousand dollars for the bazooka, which is more than they were willing to spend for just one weapon, so they passed on it. Ahmaud promised to come back and buy it in the future. He had big plans for it. He kept visualizing himself over and over firing the bazooka into a police station after they killed another unarmed black man. After all, this was a war without a doubt, and in a war you had to know when it was time to bring out the big guns.

"Yo, I started reading that book 'Policing the Black Man' the other day, that shit woke me up even more," Fred said.

"You think that's something, wait 'til you read that 'New Jim Crow.' These crackers have had us locked in a system of perpetual oppression and slavery ever since day one. When slavery supposedly ended, crackers passed a law called the Thirteenth Amendment. This law states that no one can be subjected to slavery unless they were convicted of a crime... And guess what they did after that?"

"What?" Breonna said.

"They started passing all kinds of laws so that they could re-enslave the former slaves. It's called mass incarceration today."

"That's some fucked up shit," she said.

"I know, right," Eric said.

"Can you imagine going to prison for breaking a law you didn't even know existed?" George asked.

"Most slaves couldn't even read back then"

"Exactly."

"These some dirty muthahfuckahs, word up."

"You feel me?"

"I gave y'all those books, so you'll understand what we're up against, and why we do what we do," George said.

"And we appreciate it. I damn sure was blind until I started reading those books, now I can't seem to put 'em down," Trayvon said.

"Me too."

"That's ah fact."

"Word."

"It was time for us to wake up. Everything happens for a reason," Breonna said.

"No doubt," Daunte said.

"We need some more books."

"Real talk."

"I'll see what I can do," George said.

"I wish more brothers and sisters would read these books. If more of us was aware of what was going on, these muthahfuck-ahs couldn't oppress us so easily," Andrew said.

"That's ah fact!"

"Big facts," Trayvon said.

Everything was calm and collect for the next three and one-half months. Then suddenly it happened again, back-to-back. The police killed two more unarmed black men and it was on.

On this particular night in Brooklyn, New York, Louis Jones was in a rush. He was on his way to a wedding, and he was running late. This was a big night for him. He was about to marry the woman of his life and all he could think about was the beautiful life that they were going to have together. When Lisa came into his life he thought that it was the greatest thing that ever happened to him. She's so lovely and soft spoken. She was smart and sexy. And she had one of the most magnificent bodies he'd ever seen. It was love at first sight as far as he was concerned. Soon as he saw her something inside him screamed "that's the one." And from that day on he'd been overwhelmingly attracted to her. It's like they were meant to be together. It almost seemed like a dream. And the sex – oh my god. She was an animal in the bed. The way she begged for it, then cried when he beat it up made his dick hard just thinking about it. He couldn't wait for the honeymoon.

"I don't believe this shit! I'm late for my own wedding. . . Damnit," he yelled banging his hands on the steering wheel. New York traffic had to be the worst in the world. Everything moved at the pace of a snail for it to be one of the busiest cities in the world. . . He was sitting at a red light tapping his fingers impatiently on the steering wheel when the light turned green. Making a right turn onto 108 Street where his wedding was taking place less than a block away he stepped on the gas.

As soon as his cell phone began to ring he already knew who it was. He glanced for a second and saw the woman that he loved face light up the screen of his phone. Before he could answer it, he glanced up just in time to see the big crown Vic looming ahead of him, before he crashed into the back of it. The impact caused his head to smack the steering wheel where a gash immediately opened up.

Before he could recover, several men jumped out of the car he just rear-ended and opened fire.

"Bong! "Bong!

Unknowingly Lewis had crashed his car into the back of an undercover police vehicle that was conducting a stakeout on the building about five-hundred feet from where he was to be married. A total of forty-one shots were fired into Louis' car killing him instantly. The cops claimed that they were in fear for their lives, and that they thought Lewis was one of the criminals connected to the investigation.

The police that murdered Lewis were not charged.

When the people at the wedding came out to see what was going on Lisa began screaming when she saw Louis bullet riddled car.

❖ ❖ ❖

Eurie Martin, a black man with a history of mental health issues, was walking down the street headed to his sister's house on a bright sunny afternoon. It was hot. The temperature was about one hundred three degrees, and he was thirsty. He was about twenty-five miles from the group home where he stayed, and he'd been walking all morning.

"Hooooo, it's hot as hell," he said, as he paused for a second to fan himself with his sweaty baseball cap. He looked up, shielding his eyes from the sun. He could feel the sweat trickling down his back as his dingy shirt stuck to his skin. He saw a white man in his driveway washing his car and he walked up to him with a cut off coke can in his hand.

"Hey, can I have some water please?," Eurie said motioning with the can.

"No!," the white man said turning red with anger. Eurie Was taken aback as he walked away and continued on his way to his sister's house. The white man immediately called the police after Eurie walked away.

"Nine-one-one, what's your emergency?"

"There's some black guy walking down the road, and he just came to my house and threatened me with a cut off coke can."

"Can you describe him?"

"Yeah, he looks like a monkey. He's dark skin, tall, and he got big lips. He's wearing a baseball hat, and dingy brown shirt, and blue jeans." Moments later two police cars responded, and they immediately jumped out of their cars and pulled out their tasers.

"Freeze! Put your hands above your head and get on the ground now!," screamed Officer Howell. Eurie was shocked. He didn't know what was going on or why the police were stopping him.

"Leave me alone. I haven't done anything wrong," Eurie said throwing down the coke can and taking a defensive stance.

"Get on the ground now!" Officer Copeland screamed raising his taser and pointing it at Eurie's chest.

"I ain't did nothing," Eurie said.

When Eurie failed to put his hands above his head and get on the ground, Copeland shot him with his Taser. Eurie fell to the ground, pulled the Taser prongs from his chest, got back up and tried to walk away. Howell radioed for backup. Officer Scott arrived.

"We've already tased him, but he keeps resisting," Copeland said.

"Is that right? Well let's see how much juice this nigger can take," Scott said, pulling out his own Taser. Over a four-minute seventeen-second period, officers deployed three different Tasers at least fifteen times. They then converged on Eurie and pinned him to the ground and handcuffed him.

When they finally rolled Yuri over onto his back, Eurie was dead.

"A profound and different polarization must be brought about in line with the potential for a radically different and better society representing the actual interest of the masses of people and humanity as a whole.

"Erratically a different approach to understanding and acting on the relations and problems of society must be taken up.

"Regardless of who is occupying the seats of power, systematic discrimination and murderous oppression has persisted.

"Even as the Republican Party has become more outspoken of overt and aggressive white supremacy, it is true that the Democrats, and not only the Republican Party have presided over the oppression of black people.

"The reality is that white supremacy is built into the system of capitalism-imperialism, and neither of these ruling class parties can put an end to this even if they sincerely wanted to. The answer is revolution!

"We must establish the basis as well as the orientation to uproot and abolish white supremacy and all its' oppressive relations to our society and the world at large.

"For over two-hundred years the United States Constitution has been revered by some regarded as a nearly perfect governing document. Except – it has not been, and still is not.

"The questions yet to be determined is will it be a radical reactionary or radical revolutionary solution to this problem.

"Will it mean the reinforcing of the chains of slavery or the shattering of the most decisive links in those chains, and the opening of the possibility of realizing the complete elimination of all forms of such enslavement.

"It is the language in Section 1 of the Thirteenth Amendment that has plagued the new wave slaves in the United States since 1865, for it says, "Neither slavery nor involuntary servitude, except as a punishment for crimes where of the party shall have been duly convicted shall exist within the United States."

"This exception led many, if not all, former rebel states to enact laws primarily and specifically targeting blacks and designed to easily convict them of various crimes.

"It's called mass incarceration today.

"This is our greatest problem. This is why we're still being killed today.

"These people have designed laws to keep us enslaved forever, but that fantasy world they're living in must be shattered.

"I hate to have to be the one to tell you white people but, we are no longer your slaves, so if you will, please, get, your muthahfuckin, knee, off our necks!," Rodney King, a speaker at a Black Lives Matter rally said.

The crowd began to cheer as people smiled and pumped their fists into the air. The sound of clapping and shouting could be heard several blocks away as the people gathered together and demanded change.

"Say his name!!!!!"

"Eurie Martin!!!!!"

"Say his name!!!!!"

"Eurie Martin!!!!!"

"Say his name!!!!!"

"Eurie Martin!!!!!"

"I just don't understand it. We can't even walk down the street peacefully without being killed by the police. Do they really believe that we're all scared and that we don't got the will to fight back? Well if that's what they think, then they better think again because we're tired of this shit! . . . Now we're out here, and we're trying to be as civil as we can. But it seems the more civil that we are the more bodies pile up. Now, you see what happened in Los Angeles. That's what's coming . . . I can see it as plain as day. Easy as one, two, three, A, B, C. The time limit for being nonviolent is running out. Why? . . . Because the more nonviolent we are the more violent they get. . . now I'm not promoting violence, but I be damned if I'm just going to lay down and let ah muthahfuckah think he got the right to kill me because of the color of my skin, y'all feel me-?"

The crowd began to roar. There was so much energy you could feel it vibrating through your bones. It was packed. Thousands of people were attending the rally. Sometimes they were peaceful, sometimes things got smashed and burned to the ground, depending on the atmosphere. Sometimes the speakers at the rallies would reveal so much of America's ugly truth that some people would lose control of their emotions and start taring shit up. it was very understandable considering the facts. Oppression was known to make some people do some crazy things.

Significantly meaning that yesterday this was a nation where white people were the majority, and today it is one where they are not. In a world where today's divisions are more rural versus urban than strictly South versus North. It is the case that the old and the new Confederates - and in particular rural white southerners, remain the anchor for an ill-founded and ill-intended attempt to restore the past in the name of "Making America Great Again."

This is a direct line from the confederacy to the fascist of today and a direct connection between their white supremacy and there open hatred and disgust for black and brown communities.

"Please give a round of applause for our next speaker, Mr. Troy L. Love," Lisa Edwards, one of the rally's organizers said.

"Thank you! I'm so happy that all y'all could make it today. There's no question that we're definitely out here for a reason. The forces fighting for the past are aiming to reverse, with a vengeance, even the modest concessions that have been made to fight against social injustice and institutionalized inequality and oppression. In their aim to enforce a form of capitalist dictatorship that is overt and unrestrained by the Constitution and the Rule of Law, or which turns the Constitution and the Rule of Law into a license for tyranny and atrocities at our expense, we are being killed at a steady rate with no accountability or regard.

"My question today is what is our remedy? What must we do to stop these killings of our unarmed men, women and children? Tell me, who has given them the right to value our lives as less than worthless? Where is our help? When we protest against these injustices, the National Guard doesn't show up to support us, they come to reinforce and suppress our will to live, by show of military might. They stand with our oppressors!

"This makes our situation look hopeless. It makes them seem almost invincible, doesn't it?

"Well, I stand before you today to tell you that they're not. They bleed just like we bleed. They die just like we die. Michael Johnson was a prime example of what the future looks like for those who think that they're going to continue to oppress us with impunity.

"Picture a half ah million Michael Johnsons, or a few million, then you'll be able to see what I see. As we – "

There was a commotion among the crowd. A shout of panic arose suddenly. A woman screamed as an SUV turned the corner towards the crowd of protesters and accelerated. People began to run and scatter in all directions, but it was too late. The SUV slammed into a crowd of protesters traveling at nearly seventy miles per hour. Nine people were killed instantly, sixteen more were seriously injured. Protesters immediately pulled the driver from the SUV and began beating him. Dead bodies and the injured lay on the ground side by side as several people began calling nine-one-one for medical assistance.

"Somebody call an ambulance!," A protester screamed.

Police that were monitoring the rally converged on the crowd of protesters that were still beating the man from the SUV that crashed into protesters and began breaking up the incident. Devin White, a twenty-three-year-old white man was taken into police custody and charged with nine counts of murder and sixteen counts of attempted murder, and aggravated assault with a deadly weapon with intent to kill and inflicting serious injury.

Two days later police investigators linked Devon White to a white supremacist nationalist group called the Pride Boys after searching his parents' home in Tate, Mississippi.

CHAPTER 20

DOMESTIC TERRORISM

After the domestic terrorist attack at the Black Lives Matter rally in Tate, Mississippi, George and the crew decided to go back and buy the bazooka from their Mexican gun dealer, and they didn't hesitate to use it either . . . . . .

Seven days later Ahmaud arrived in Mississippi driving a beat-up, old black van with a rusty tail pipe and the paint peeling from the passenger's side door in several areas.

He was dressed in a simple disguise, just a little makeup and a Jerry curl wig; Black jeans, black sweater, black Timberland boots. He was also wearing a surgical mask which looked like shark teeth all around.

He was more than a little bit nervous. He was probably the only black man in the United States ridding around with a bazooka, as a matter of fact. He kept looking over his shoulder to where it was currently resting, rolled up in a thick brown rug.

On the seat next to him lay a fully automatic weapon with a one hundred round drum underneath a beach towel which read in huge letters, "Make America Great Again."

He was wearing a bulletproof vest.

There's no question that he was definitely dressed for the occasion.

He checked his rearview mirror again to make sure no cops were behind him. He'd already decided that if any cops pulled him over that he was going to hop out and start spraying shit, no questions asked. The only thing he had on his mind was revenge, there was little room for anything else. He checked his watch. He entered the Tate County city limits a little after seven o'clock and went straight to the nearest hotel. There, he bought a room, kicked up his feet, turned on the news and waited. In two days Devin White was scheduled for his first court appearance, and Ahmaud vowed to show up with the judge and jury to make sure he got a fair trial.

To emphasize this crucial point, it is necessary to confront the fundamental reality, that there is no future worth living for the masses of black people. And ultimately for humanity as a whole, under a system of oppression which continues to multiply the unmitigated juggernaut of horrors which poses a threat to their very existence(s).

The fact that there is no bringing back an idealized way of life that's supposedly existed in the late 19th century and the first part of the 20th century in this country. No return to an imagined idyllic America characterized by traditional values of slaves and slave masters - something which has always existed only in the minds of those who seek an illusionary restoration of this, and who have been conditioned to irrationally hate everyone and everything that has supposedly destroyed it.

A future lies not with the real or imagined past, but in going forward. Where the fundamental orientation and practical policies are geared to meeting the material intellectual and cultural values and needs of the people, while giving increasing scope to individual initiative on the basis of and within the framework of the collective and cooperative foundation as ethos of society. Where age-old economic and social relations of exploitation, inequality and oppression are surpassed, and no longer does the well-being of the few rest on the misery of the many.

It should be clear enough that the present polarization and the profound problems that must be faced cannot be solved by trying to adjust within the confines of a system of oppression.

It must be opposed by all means necessary.

For more than four-hundred years blacks were forced to conform to a system of hate, discrimination and racism, subjected to continual terror, marked by repeated lynchings and other depraved acts of violence and brutality.

But unfortunately, like so many other systems of oppression, this one had also run its course. A new breed of men were being birth due to these horrendous conditions which had existed for far too long.

And it's the same reason Ahmaud was parked across the street from the Tate County Jail at six-forty-five on this beautiful chilly spring morning.

He was about to demonstrate why and how white supremacy would no longer be tolerated by those who had been its victims for centuries. The price for doing business as usual had just went up. And the stakes were high as ever. Ahmaud climbed into the back of the van and began unrolling the bazooka from the rug. He had two rockets. One was already cocked and loaded, and the other was laying on the unfolded rug beside him.

He was ready. He lay down on the rug beside the bazooka and closed his eyes for a few seconds.

"Michael Johnson, you's ah bad muthahfuckah," Ahmaud said. He opened his eyes.

Peeking out the back window of the van he saw extra police cars begin to arrive at the jail.

"Show time," he said, "menace to society."

Across the street about a dozen officers were standing on the steps of the jail waiting for the prisoner Devin White, who they were assigned to escort to the Tate County Courthouse for his first appearance.

Dressed in an orange jumpsuit with County Jail written in large black letters on the back, Devin White, escorted by four sheriff deputies appeared at the front entrance of the jail and began to descend the steps towards the waiting SUV police vehicle. Immediately the twelve officers standing in front of the jail surrounded him. He was wearing two bullet proof vests and a police tactical helmet on his head. He had a smile on his face like he was America's greatest hero or something. He had his head held high like he didn't have a care in the world. He was proud of himself.

As Devin was being led to the SUV he just happened to look across the street just in time to see Ahmaud open up the rear doors of the van and step out with the bazooka. The first thought that came to his mind as the smile disappeared from his face was "that can't be real." He froze. He tried to turn as several officers shoved him forward. That's when he heard a sound like air being compressed before his body was blown into a million pieces.

Thirteen of the sixteen cops surrounding Devin White died instantly. The other three would never work again as police officers. Two of them lost both of their legs and the other one lost one of his legs and both of his arms. One cop totally engulfed in flames tried to run back into the jail. He died gripping the door handle as his flesh continued to cook and melt.

Ahmaud didn't even blink. He loaded the second rocket and fired into the front entrance of the jail as the other officers were attempting to come to the aid of their fellow officers, killing six more officers.

The scene looked like something out of a World War II movie.

Twisted vehicles and thick black smoke was the reality of the situation which only moments ago seemed so calm.

Ahmaud jumped behind the wheel of the van then fled, leaving behind a nightmare in his wake.

He was less than four blocks away when he found himself being pursued by several police cars. The two video cameras on top of the jail had recorded the entire incident. The sheriff deputy monitoring the footage was already screaming for help before Ahmaud fixed the first rocket, but by the time the officers heard the warning it was too late, he'd already pulled the trigger. And took out their whole squad. Ahmaud looked in his rearview mirror. He saw two police cars behind him. Then it was three, then it turned into five. Then seven. Then ten. He reached over to the passenger seat and uncovered the machine gun. He smiled as he mashed the gas pedal to the floor. He wished that he had another rocket left so he could really go out with a bang.

He turned a corner so fast the van was literally on two wheels for a split second. No matter what he did he couldn't seem to shake his pursuers.

He glanced in his rearview mirror again and it seemed like every Police Department in the state was behind him.

He wasn't afraid at all.

This was a sacrifice centuries in the making and he was more than willing.

But two things for sure and one thing for certain, they were definitely not going to take him alive. Hands down. No questions asked.

"In our exclusive breaking NEWS UPDATE –

"Police are currently involved in a high speed chase in Tate County, Mississippi where a suspect armed with a rocket propelled grenade launcher ambushed police as they were escorting Devin White, the suspect accused of driving his SUV into a crowd of protesters at a Black Lives Matter rally, to his first court appearance at the Tate County Courthouse early this morning.

"According to an unidentified police source, Devin White, along with more than a dozen officers, were killed when the suspect fired two rockets at them as they were attempting to load Devin White into a police vehicle in front of the Tate County jail.

"Video footage from the jail's surveillance cameras shows this man climbing from the rear doors of a van parked across the street from the jail and firing the weapon.

"So far the suspect has not been identified," the news broadcaster said.

"That's him, isn't it?," Breonna said in a whisper.

"You already know," George said as they watched the surveillance photos of Ahmaud continue to flash back and forth from the high speed chase in progress, to the destruction caused by the explosions. Breonna squeezed George's hand tighter as tears began to run down her face.

Ahmaud continued to drive like a madman as he weaved back and forth in and out of traffic. It was useless. He wasn't going to be able to shake his pursuers.

It was time to make a stand.

Looking in his rearview mirror he saw one of the cop cars creeping up beside him getting ready to ram him and try to run him off the road. He picked up the machine gun and set it on his lap. He rolled the window down. Just as soon as the patrol car got just about even with him, he stuck the machine gun halfway out the window and let it rip.

"Say hellow to my little friend," Ahmaud said as he pulled the trigger and sent a burst of about eight bullets into the roof of the squad car.

"GUAH! GUAH! GUAH! GUAH! GUAH! GUAH! GUAH! GUAH!" The powerful machine gun roared. One of the bullets ripped through the top of the officer's head just above his ear and blew a big gaping hole through the bottom of his chin. Immediately the squad car swerved out of control and hit a parked car and flipped about three times before coming to a rest on its side. Ahmaud didn't even look back.

One of the van's back windows blew out. They were shooting at him. He ducked his head when he heard the window explode and glass ran down onto the floor of the van. He made a hard right, then a hard left. Then another hard right. Tires spinning. Rubber burning.

He was like a man possessed.

All he needed to do was shake them for a few good seconds and he was going to try to pull a stunt.

He already formulated a plan in his head of exactly what he was going to do. Even though the chances of success was extremely low for what he was planning to do, he figured what did he have to lose, either way it was over for him.

The light up ahead turned red and he decided that now was the time. He pressed his foot to the gas and ran the red light. He barely made it through the break in traffic, a split second late and he would have plowed into an eighteen wheeler doing over one-hundred miles per hour.

Unfortunately the cop cars trailing him were not so lucky. Three of them crashed, killing one officer and seriously injuring two more.

The accident caused a major pileup.

The gods must have been looking down on him and answered his prayers. It was the break he needed.

He turned left, drove about two more blocks, turned right and park the van in an alley.

Quickly he grabbed the gas can that he brought with him, poured gas all over the van, then set it on fire.

Grabbing the backpack containing his clothes, he put the machine gun in the bag and took off running.

He could hear the police sirens coming from, it seemed like, everywhere.

Pulling off his mask and wig he dipped into a clothing store and blended in.

"Excuse me sir," a clerk said walking up to him.

Ahmaud almost shitted on himself.

"Yes?" Ahmaud said.

"Didn't you see the sign? You have to wear a mask on these premises. I know it's a bunch of bull, but these are the CDC rules. Remember your three W's. Sorry sir," the clerk said.

"Damn, my bad. I almost forgot. Do you have one I can buy?," Ahmaud asked.

"You don't have to buy one sir, we hand out free ones to all our customers that need one. . . here you go," the clerk said handing Ahmaud the mask, smiling.

"Thanks," Ahmaud said returning his smile.

"No problem."

A cop car flew by.

Ahmaud tried to remain as calm as possible. He bought a few items. Went into the dressing room and changed clothes, put his backpack on and walked outside. He looked up. It was a beautiful day. Clear blue skies, sun shining bright. He started walking down the sidewalk. He just kept walking like nothing even happened. A few cop cars flew past him, but he pretended not to notice and just kept on walking.

He pulled the new baseball hat down tightly over his head, adjusted his mask, and kept right on walking. He stopped at a fast food restaurant, ordered two burgers, two fries and a large soda. And as he ate his burger and fries he continued to walk.

Before he realized it, he'd walked about five and one-half miles. He stopped when he came upon a Motel 6. He bought a room for five days, put the "Do not disturb" sign on the door, went in and fell asleep. He didn't come out the room for three days. All he did was watch the news and sleep. The person they were looking for didn't exist. He'd watch the news about one hundred times over the last three days making sure of that.

On the fourth day he left the motel and made his way back to North Carolina.

He had a story to tell . . . . For some reason he was convinced that he had to be the luckiest muthahfuckah in the world. That's ah fact.

A grand game of chess is being played on a level that we can only imagine, and we are the pawns. Pawns are valuable pieces only under certain circumstances and are frequently sacrificed to gain the strongest advantage possible.

How can we survive any longer by holding onto the falsehoods of the past?

Reality must be discerned at all costs if we are to be a part of a quickly approaching future. Clinging to the past is guaranteed destruction like remaining apathetic is assured genocidal enslavement. If we do not act in consent with each other and overcome the system of discrimination and racism to ensure that the future becomes what we need it to be, then surely we deserve whatever fate awaits us to come.

Black Vigilante. The Executioners.

CHAPTER 21

SEX AND BLACK LIVES MATTER

The Constitution of the United States of America, in the Declaration of Independence and the fully recognized and acknowledged historical facts that have served as the justification for the destruction of tyrants proceeds us.

"In this world where blatant acts of the miscarriage of justice are the norm, and racism has reached an astronomical scale, an issue of primary concern arises.

"Consequently, in the interest of future world order, sincere peace and tranquility, an ultimate objective must be concluded by those who have suffered under the weight of oppression for centuries. In conclusion, the objective be simple – give me liberty, or give me death.

"We must not be distracted or confused with matters of no real importance on the other hand. This process begins with a clear and candid description of why we're here, as we begin to explore this tentative definition with maximum certainty.

"It's called oppression.

"God knows we've had our share of it in this country, to no end.

"Who can deny these self-evident truths? If any ignore these truths it is because they an indictment of their own ignorance that they cannot face.

"But even so, these truths cannot be negated. The message is clear – You must accept that you have been the focus of centuries of oppression and slavery, and you must prepare to fight, and if necessary, die to preserve our God given right to freedom and existence. If you don't believe in racism by now, you're a fool, because millions do, and their beliefs, and actions based on those beliefs, affect us significantly.

"No, we cannot fight against our oppressors with conventional weapons and standing armies, because for every car or truck we have they have a thousand tanks and Humvees. And for a every gun we have they probably got a million.

"But what we do have is more and more brothers and sisters willing to be the next Michael Johnson, a radical form of thinking that's being birth from the womb of hate, discrimination, racism and oppression. White people call us terrorists and pretend like they don't know or understand why these things are happening.

"Please. Stop fooling yourselves.

"These muthahfuckahs done rewrote history so much that they don't even know what the fuck is going on anymore.

"Well, let me explain. It's called suppression. You've lost the ability to suppress the pain. You're under the impression that you're still living in the Eighteenth Century and still riding around on wagons and shit. This is the information age. Knowledge travels at the speed of light; a touch of a button. Even though y'all may have changed the name lynching to "Police killings" and stand your ground, it's still lynchings. Just because you've switched up your methods to using guns and tasers instead of ropes, it's still lynching.

"My point is this – Now when someone is lynched it's not just an incident confined to that immediate area or state where it happen. The whole Goddamn world can see it now. The pain and reality of oppression is felt for thousands of miles in every direction. Tell me, who in the hell wants to live in a society where they're being constantly killed and oppressed by their own government because of the color of their skin?

"We ain't walking around killing white people because they're white; and these muthahfuckahs raped, kidnapped and murdered us for centuries.

"Let me attempt to quote to you the scenario which is developing right before your eyes because I refuse to let you pretend like you don't grasp the truth of what's happening, and why it's happening. It may be true that we cannot face America's armies, but you'll be virtually powerless to defend against hundreds of thousands of individual acts of retaliation.

"Has it yet become apparent that one attacker fueled by centuries of hate and oppression can cause (the) destruction as if he were a thousand men? Please don't take my speech out of context because I'm not standing up here promoting violence or hate. I'm explaining to you the facts of how violence and hate got us to where we are today."

Another rally had jumped off in Rocky Mount, North Carolina, and the event was twice as big as the last one.

The speaker, John Lewis, an old civil rights movement activists was putting it down again. He'd been traveling all over the United States for the past two months holding rally after rally and it didn't look like he had any intentions of stopping anytime soon.

"He sounds like the next Malcolm X," Breonna said.

"He was doing this shit way before Malcom X was," George replied.

"Well he sure hasn't lost his touch."

"That's ah fact!"

"Have you heard from Ahmaud yet?"

"Yeah, he sent me a message by Eric. . . said he was going to lay low for a few months."

"He's lucky to be alive. I don't know how he did it, but he made it."

"That's ah fact."

"When I saw what he was up against I cried and prayed for him."

"Well what ever you told God it must have been convincing."

"I think so."

"Me too," George said reaching for her hand.

"I think we should celebrate."

"That sounds like a good idea. What do you want to do?" he asked.

Breonna whispered in his ear, "How bout a lot of suckin and fuckin," she said smiling. She licked his ear.

His dick started to get hard just thinking about it. She noticed the lump in the front of his pants. She smiled again as she felt the heat rise between her legs.

After the rally was over they drove back to George's house. There was a lot of kissing and touching at every red light, and in between. They had finally decided to live together, and to both of them it was like a dream come true. They just couldn't seem to get enough of each other.

After pulling into the driveway George got out the car, came around and opened the door for her. He then picked her up and carried her into the house. He never could help admiring how soft she felt in his hands. It always made his dick get hard nearly every time he touched her.

He carried her to his bed and slung her to the center where she bounced up and down like she was on a small trampoline.

"You on some cave man shit ain'tcha?," she said smiling wickedly.

He wasn't smiling. He had a serious look on his face. He was dead ass. aggressively he began to pull off her clothes. In the process her bra popped, and her panties got ripped. Rolling her over onto her stomach George snatched her panties the rest of the way off, tearing them again. He wanted her so bad; the desire was overwhelming. With every move he made on the bed her ass would sway with the motion. He couldn't take his eyes off of it.

It seemed like his clothes melted away; he couldn't remember, all he knew was that he was suddenly naked with a throbbing erection that needed attention.

Pulling the folds of her luscious ass open with his thumbs he became even more excited when he saw those two fat pussy lips poking out, smiling at him. He licked across the sensitive buds.

Breonna moaned in pleasure.

He kissed them.

He sucked them.

He pulled on them with this lips.

"Ooooh! . . . . Ooooh God!" she moaned as George began to push his tongue slowly between her slippery folds. The pleasure was unbelievable. It seemed like every time he made love to her he took her to newer heights.

Repeatedly George plunged his tongue into the pussy. He enjoyed the taste of her. The smell of her pussy mixed with her perfume was trance-like.

He sucked the pussy real hard then stabbed his tongue into it deep. Breonna began to tremble and shake with her first orgasm.

"Ooooh! . . . It's cumin! Ooooh God it's cumin!," She moaned as she began to shake uncontrollably.

Breonna reached back with both hands and held the pussy and ass open for him, as the tremors continued to convulse through her body. Her sticky liquids began to flow as George continued to feast on her tender flesh. His face looked like he was wearing a little bit of shaving cream. George stuck the tip of his tongue in her asshole and wiggled it in a circular motion. Breonna came again instantly.

"See, why you doin me like this, oh yeeees! . . . It's so good! . . . It's so good," she cried as her body continued to tremble and shake.

"You like that baby? . . . You like that?," George said as he began to dig in the pussy with his fingers.

"Yessss," she moaned.

He liked the way she sounded. So gentle. So sweet.

He played in the pussy some more.

He licked it again, dragging his tongue slowly over her love tunnel.

She was still holding the pussy open for him.

He climbed on top of her and fell in the pussy, like a soldier falling on his sword. Breonna gasped when she felt her cunt lips split apart and engulf the long, thick, juicy black dick.

"AAAAAAugh!," she cried out every time he stabbed her with is spear. "AAAAAugh!"

He rode her hard and fast.

It sounded like someone was clapping their hands every time he plowed into her silky warmth.

"Smack! Smack! Smack! Smack! Smack! Smack! Smack! Smack! Smack!," groans and moans, as he continued to beat the pussy up.

Every time he drilled the dick into her he thought of hot butter melting.

He felt like he was in another world which was filled with nothing but pleasure.

He slowed down.

He sped up.

He grinded on it.

He twisted his hips in a circular motion.

He plowed into the pussy from a right angle for thirty to forty strokes.

Then he spanked the pussy from the left angle for another forty to fifty strokes.

"UNAAAAAugh! . . . UNAAAAAugh! . . . UNAAAAAugh!" Breonna moaned every time he slammed into the pussy. She lost count of her orgasms. She was keeping up with them. After the sixth one she lost count and couldn't remember nothing but the good dick he was giving her.

Sweat was pouring off of him, dripping onto her back. The warm droplets seemed to excite her even more as they ran down her back.

"You fuckin me this good. . . Oh God . . . I ain't never been done like this," she moaned in that sweet little girl's voice, that always turned him on.

Grabbing her around the hips he jerked her ass high into the air and began fucking her hard and fast.

"Smack! Smack! Smack! Smack! Smack! Smack!," is what it sounded like every time he hit her. "UAgh! . . . UAgh!," George groaned as he held her hips tightly and forced her to take his beastly thrusts.

That feeling suddenly came over him. He could feel the heat rising deep within his balls. He began to pound harder and faster. Breonna fell back onto her stomach. George fell on top of her. He was like a man possessed. As he pressed down on her shoulders convulsing, he emptied his seed inside her while they both moaned and groaned together in overwhelming pleasure.

"You showed your ass a little while ago didn't yah?," Breonna said as she lay on the bed with her face resting on her hand watching him.

"Girl, what you talkin bout," George replied, playing innocent.

"I'm talking about you. Beatin the pussy up like Mike Tyson," Breonna said smiling.

George had a big shit-eatin grin on his face. He was well aware that he had worked his magic on her. Her acknowledgment of the fact had him feeling himself even more.

"Well you know . . . A man's gottah do what ah man's gottah do," he said smiling.

"I know that's right. . . This pussy still tingling and throbbing . . . I gottah keep my eyes on you," she said rolling her eyes playfully.

"Bre what you talking bout?" he said.

"I gottah make sure you don't give my stuff away. You know how to make a bitch fall in love."

"I'm glad you think so highly of me."

"Hump."

"Don't worry Bae, you don't got nothing to worry about."

"I don't?"

"Not at all," he said leaning over and kissing her gently on the lips.

She kissed him back. Then she kissed him some more. Within moments they were tongue fucking each other's mouth until they were out of breath.

They were laying on the bed still naked. It didn't take long for things to start heating up again.

Breonna laid her upper body across his stomach. She caressed his meaty lump of flesh which was only semi-hard. She put her mouth on it and pulled on the head of it with her lips. She liked to play with it while it was still soft. She liked to watch how it growed hard and stiff in her little hands. It was so amazing.

She kissed it.

"AAAugh!," George groaned.

She smiled. She loved to bring him pleasure.

She stuck her tongue out and slowly began to lick around the head of his pole.

She took her time.

There was no need to rush.

"Shit!," George said when she crammed a huge chunk of his meat in her mouth and began applying suction-cup-like pressure.

He damn near jumped off the bed.

He loved watching her perform. It was captivating. "Suck it! . . . Oh God, suck it Bee!," he groaned as he played in her hair with his hand.

Eyes rolling back into his head, head moving from side to side George was trapped in total bliss as he was literally eaten alive.

Once Breonna started deep throating the dick and making those choking sounds in the back of her throat it was over for him.

"AAAAugh! . . . AAAAAugh! . . . Shiiiit! AAAAAugh!," George grunted as he pumped his seed down her throat.

Placing his hands on the back of her head, George held her down on him as he continued to jerk and twitch as he coated her throat with cum juice.

Finally Breonna pulled the long dick from her mouth.

"Damn man, you almost strangled me," she said gasping for breath. She smiled, then licked the last few drops of cum from his one eye monster.

George was still breathing heavily. He just laid there because he thought he probably couldn't stand right now anyway if he tried to.

"Im'ah have to keep my eyes on you . . . make sure you don't give my stuff away . . . You know how to make a muthahfuckah fall in love," George said, repeating the same thing she had told him a little while ago. He had that look in his eyes.

Breonna was smiling.

She leaned over and kissed his nut sack.

"You don't got nothin to worry about babe. This your pussy," she said as she slowly began licking and sucking on his balls.

The dick got hard again instantly.

It was on again.

CHAPTER 22

LABEL ME

Police in Tate County, Mississippi, have been conducting door to door searches seeking any information that would lead to the where abouts and arrest of the suspect who ambushed police at the Tate County Jail one week ago today. A total of nineteen police were killed in that attack along with the man accused of ramming his vehicle into a crowd of Black Lives Matter supporters who were protesting the recent killing of an unarmed black man by police.

Video footage from the Tate County Jail's surveillance cameras shows a man exiting the back of a van parked across the street from the jail, firing a weapon that police have identified as being a bazooka, into a crowd of police who were escorting Devin White to the Tate County Court House for his first appearance. Several officers were badly injured.

During a high speed chase immediately after the attack, two other officers were killed while trying to apprehend the suspect.

One officer was killed when the suspect opened fire with an automatic weapon, and the other was killed when his cruiser plowed into the side of an eighteen wheeler during the chase.

Several officers were also injured in that incident.

Seemingly the suspect managed to escape and is believed to still be hiding somewhere in the area.

In an exclusive police interview Police Chief Tim Scott, the State's first and only African America to hold the position, had this to say to reporters –

"The Tate County Police Department and the State of Mississippi have considered this recent cowardly attack to be a vicious act of terrorism, and we will not rest until those who are responsible are brought to justice. Personally I feel like elements of the Black Lives Matter movement are somehow involved in these blatant attacks that have been recently occurring over the United States."

"Chief Scott, do you have any proof of that?," a young reporter asked.

"I have my reasons . . . Angry black men and women are being convinced that the entire criminal justice system is inherently racist at these rallies, and they're being encouraged to retaliate against law enforcement. These people have to be stopped. I think all Black Lives Matter gatherings should be considered unlawful assemblies in this country because it teaches that America is a racist country which is not true."

Many in the black community were shocked at Chief Scott's statements. Others were not surprised at all. Most considered him to be a house nigger just doing what a house nigger has been trained to do for centuries.

"Those responsible will be held accountable for their actions accordingly. And we will not rest a single day or spare a single resource until the perpetrators are caught. Currently all our departments are working closely with the F.B.I. and other law enforcement agencies to track down these killers. These people are a disgrace to our great society, and they will not get away with this.

"At this time I would like to express my deep condolences to the families of the officers who were lost or wounded during this tragic event. Please rest assure that we are going to do everything we can to bring you the closure you deserve. I understand, and I feel your pain."

"Chief Scott, do you know how the suspect was able to escape?"

"We have reason to believe that he may have had help. The investigation is ongoing," he said.

"Chief Scott, do you think the State will seek the death penalty once the suspect is caught?"

"I would . . . No further questions."

"Chief Scott –"

"Chief Scott –"

Chief Scott left the podium and disappeared back into the building, where he headed straight for his office. He was mad as hell. Embarrassed, and disappointed, he kept wondering over and over in his head, "How did this muthahfuckah get away with over half the Goddamn department on his heels?" he just couldn't believe it. He wanted to hold somebody responsible, but now definitely wasn't the time.

During the year 2020 the government of the United States was confronted with a series of events which were to change beyond prediction it's future and the future of humanity itself. These events were so incredible that they stunned the entire world.

A global pandemic, mass social unrest, and the possible sightings of alien spacecrafts were at the top of the list.

Foreign and Military Agencies formed a Select Committee to study government operations through a directive by Congress which empowered the Secretary of State to coordinate information and activities designed to counter communism. Initial authority was given to the CIA for covert operations, established formal procedures for either coordinating or approving these operations.

It directed the F.B.I. to undertake covert actions and ensure through liaison with the State and Defense Departments that the resulting operations were consistent with American laws and policies.

These actions were designed to form a buffer between the operations and the president; to serve as a means for the president to deny any knowledge if leaks divulged the true state of any past or ongoing operations. The Secretary of Defense objected to this secrecy and believed that the American people should be told.

He began to talk to leaders of the opposition party concerning the matter, he was asked to resign by President Trump, the former president. Top secret government agencies infiltrated Black Lives Matters and all other social movement groups. Their aim was to disrupt the organizations and seek out those responsible for recent police killings. But with all their training, resources and technology they failed to find one single individual responsible in the attacks, and the social justice movements continued to grow. The FBI and the CIA began to use dirty tactics in order to charge demonstrators with conspiracy charges by initiating conversations in regard to killing police and government officials. Character assassinations were tools that criminal investigators used unabated and with impunity frequently.

Their attempts to neutralize certain segments of the population failed while Black Lives Matter and the truth of America's shameful history continued to expand.

Police killings of unarmed blacks and Hispanics continued, and the rise of retribution increased.

The FBI and the CIA concluded that an organized gang of terrorists were not responsible, for what seemed to be coordinating attacks against law enforcement personnel, but a loose network of vigilantes whose numbers were beginning to increase significantly due to the killings of unarmed blacks and Hispanics by police.

"Yo, we bout to switch the game up on these crackers yah heard?," George said.

"What's the dealy?," Eric asked.

They were all in attendance. Fred, Andrew, Breonna, Trayvon, Daunte, George and Eric. Everybody was there except Ahmaud, who was laying low somewhere deep in the woods with about five pounds of weed, two chicks, several cases of gin, eight ounces of coke and enough food and water to last at least six months. He was strapped with a hell of a Survival kit, and he wasn't showing his face no time soon.

"everything we do gonah be from long range from here on out. After seeing that shit that Ahmaud went through I've decided that's way too risky. We almost lost a good brother, you feel me," George said.

"Word up."

"What you mean long range?," Fred asked.

"I'm talking about high power rifles with the scope, and remote controlled bombs yah heard."

"You on some Bin Laden shit for real aint'chah."

"No doubt."

"D.C. sniper all over again," Trayvon said smiling, as he began rolling up a blunt.

"You feel me . . . . . The cops are going to step up their efforts in apprehension by shutting down wide ranges of areas, and we need enough time to get outside that bubble before that trap closes," George said.

"What made you think of that?"

"I don't know. I just been brain storming. I guess after watching millions of cop shows on T.V. it can make your mind wonder about the possibilities in situations like this," he said.

"Real talk," Trayvon said blowing out a cloud of smoke.

"What's up with those trap houses?," Andrew said.

"Business as usual . . . We caked up again," Daunte said, smiling.

"That's what's up."

"Have y'all been paying attention to the news lately? A lot of cops been getting their wigs pushed back yah-heard," Fred said.

"I know, right. We definitely ain't the only ones taking the fight to these muthahfuckahs. And it's about time," Trayvon said.

"I don't see what choice we have, because it's obvious that these muthahfuckahs don't intend to stop killing us," Fred said.

"That's ah fact!"

"I mean hell, do they think we suppose to just march forever? Enough is enough. somebody gottah show these muthahfuckahs what time it is because the clock done ran out in overtime, you feel me?," Fred said.

"Word-up."

"I feel the same way."

"Me too."

"They say you reap what you sow."

"Well, according to their Bible it says, "Do unto others as you will have them do unto you," and since they gave us this Bible and told us that this was the word of God, I'm just doing the work of my savior," Daunte said, smiling.

"Amen to that," Breonna said.

"Preach Paster."

"Can I get a witness?"

"Thank you Jesus."

"The way I see it, I'm just casting out devils, you feel me," Daunte said.

"Word," Trayvon replied in agreement.

"Yo, excuse me my brother, but if you don't mind will you please pass that blunt? Damn! You be babysittin the shit. We like to smoke too, you feel me?" Fred said.

"You know how he get when he get tah talking," Breonna said, rolling her eyes.

"Man, fuck that shit. Y'all always cryin. Talkin bout I be baby sittin the blunt. Matter of fact, here, roll your own fucking blunts." Trayvon said, tossing a sack of weed on the table. Breonna slapped him on the back of the head, and he started coughing smoke uncontrollably.

They all started laughing.

"A yo, I finished that book "The Exhuming of A Nation," That shit is amazing, and it all makes perfect sense. I ain't never read no shit like that in my life. I learned more about myself and my people in that one book than I've learned from every book I've ever read since I've been on this earth, put together."

"Say word."

"On everything I love," Andrew said.

"Let me read it next," Breonna said.

"I got you. I got it in the car. Just remind me to give it to you before I dipp."

"Why don't you go get it now, so we don't have to worry about that," she said crossing her arms over her breast.

Fred got up and went to his car to get the book for her. Moments later he came back and handed it to her.

"Thanks!" she said. She opened up the book and started reading it as she rolled herself a blunt. It didn't take long before she was captivated.

"Yo this some deep shit," she said after reading only a few pages.

"You ain't even seen the half yet," Fred replied.

"Hey when are you planning on seeing our Mexican?," Andrew asked.

"I was thinking maybe we should chill for about a month before we buss our next move. Shit real hot right now wit this police shit and I think it'll be wise to fall-back for a little while," George said.

"That's a good idea. Ain't nothing wrong with playing it safe and following you instincts," Breonna said.

They were all in agreement.

"I know that we done sat up in here and had this same conversation before but ain't ah damn thing changed. As long as they continue to kill us, we'll continue to kill them. I don't give a fuck if they get the F.B.I., the CIA, A.B.C. or D.F.G. H.I.J.K.L.M.N.O.P. We gon ride on these muthahfuckahs you feel me," George said.

"Word-up!"

"It's on like that!"

"Really tho!"

"Once they realize that there's going to be repercussions for their hateful actions, things will change," George said.

"I know that's right."

"You better believe it."

"The tide is already turning against them," he said.

CHAPTER 23

EXECUTIONER

Violent behaviors are a sequence of emotions and actions that are learned. More than eighty-nine percent of violent crimes are committed by men in this country. Prisons are filled with men who have acted out in violence towards those who they felt were weaker or a threat... Or in some cases, just pure hatred.

Violent acts are triggered in many ways. And each act causes its own degree of destruction. Anger, frustration, revenge and fear are the main spring for this action. If unchecked, only God can determine the outcome.

War is also an excuse we use for violence for the purpose of conquering a foe, defending our possessions, or warding off an aggressor.

In order to achieve a desired result sometimes violence is necessary.

In the beginning of society structure men were subjected to blind and brutal forces, and afterwards to law, which is the same forces cleverly disguised.

In America, during the era of its creation, slave masters, slave-holders and slave patrollers designated themselves rulers over the black race against our wills.

They tormented us.

Brutalized us.

Molested our children.

Raped our women with impunity.

For centuries you lynched us.

You chopped off our hands and feet.

You beat us unmercifully.

You taught us to fear you.

You told us we were criminals.

You mis-educated us.

These same violent men made themselves our overseers.

They vowed to keep us in chains and make us their slaves forever.

They called themselves lawmen and they wrote laws designed to imprison us.

They built thousands and thousands of courts and jails.

They kidnapped us.

These same violent men concocted a plan they called it the criminal justice system. A systematically racist organization that was anything but just.

They truly believed that centuries of programming by slave masters would ensure that we would maintain a slave mentality forever, but they were wrong.

But they must have been under the impression that the same violence they used to climb to the top of the world would sustained them for eternity, but they were wrong

They did their best to prepare for it.

They even erased our memories.

With the stroke of a pen they rewrote our history.

They rejoiced over us when they saw that we were asleep.

But something happened which suddenly changed the course of things.

A new world arose where people demanded a more peaceful and just society.

But these centuries-old violent men were stubborn, and still stuck in their ways, and they refused to listen.

We pleaded with them.

We begged them.

We ask them for forgiveness for sins that we did not commit.

They laughed in our face.

They disregarded our grievances.

For some strange reason these violent men took pride in seeing us suffer.

It brought them great pleasure to see us in chains.

They believed that our spirits were broken.

They were wrong.

How so?

Well you see, it was the continuing violent acts of these violent men which gave us back our souls.

Their vicious attacks caused us to wonder. We began to ask ourselves; "Why are they doing this? Why won't they stop?"

They made us dig to find the answer to these questions.

They forced to see the truth.

They forced us to face reality where we came to understand the American dream was actually our nightmare.

We were woke.

It's too late to say I'm sorry.

Love don't live here anymore.

Willie Smith was high on meth, and he'd already been up for three days. He was tired but he'd already decided that today was the day. It was now or never. The time had come for somebody to pay. Justice was going to be served. No justice. No peace.

He was parked in front of the Nash County courthouse sitting in his car snorting crystal meth and smoking Newports back-to-back.

Wrapped up in a blanket on the back seat behind him was an AR-15 that he kept referring to as Arron Rogers.

"It's just you and me Arron Rogers. We bout to win the Super Bowl. I'm ah run the route, you just throw me the bomb and I promise you I'm ah catch that muthahfuckah O.K.," he said slurring his words.

He was high out of his mind.

A woman walked by and waived at him, and he didn't even see her. She had just come out of the courthouse, and she was on her way home. Lucky for her because five minutes later she might have been dead.

Willie poured a half a gram of meth on his wrist and snorted it up his right nostril.

"AAAAAiiih," he said, tears forming in his eyes.

He poured the same amount on his writs again and snorted it up the left side, "AAAAAiiih," his ears popped. It sounded like a high frequency whistle was going off in his head. He heard a train coming.

He didn't really hear a train it was actually the effects that the drug was having on him.

Reaching into the back seat, Willie unrolled the AR-15 assault rifle from the blanket. He placed it in his lap.

He cocked it and clicked the safety off.

A Rocky Mount police officer shot his grandmother's eye out with a rubber bullet during a Black Lives Matter rally, and he'd come to repay them for it.

He got out of the car with the rifle in tow and walked up the steps of the courthouse. He opened the door and closed it behind him.

Court was in session.

Raising the gun, he ran down the middle of the aisle. As soon as the bailiff turned toward him, Willie shot him in the face from about ten feet away. Brains and blood splattered the court reporter and her typewriter. She began to scream.

Leveling the gun at the judge he shot him twice in the chest spilling him from his leather chair. He was dead before he hit the floor.

Quickly turning, Willie pointed the gun at the District Attorney and the assistant District Attorney who were trying to dodge for cover. Too late. He shot both of them several times in the back and twice in the neck killing both of them instantly.

The court reporter was still screaming so he turned around and shot her too. The court reporter stopped screaming.

Several cops that were in the building rushed to the courtroom. People were jumping over benches and chairs scrambling, trying to get the fuck out of the way. Willie didn't pay them any attention. He was here for one group of people and one group of people only. The authorities.

Officers responding to the shots rushed into the courtroom, weapons drawn. Willie opened fire soon as he seen them, cutting two officers down like plywood. A third officer shot Willie in the chest. Willie was so high he didn't even feel it, he kept firing the AR-15.

"Y'all muthahfuckahs think y'all gon'ah get away with hurting my family! . . . Im'ah kill all y'all muthahfuckahs today!," Willie screamed as he popped the empty clip out and reloaded. During the process of reloading Willie took another bullet to the chest. The cop that shot him took cover behind the jury box. Willie opened fire emptying the clip, riddling the jury box and the cop who shot him with bullet holes.

Seven cops in S.W.A.T. gear came through the same doors Willie came through and shot Willie in the back of the head.

It was over.

Willie Smith shook the Rocky Mount Police Department to the core. . . . .

Four days after the Nash County Court House shooting, police shot and killed an unarmed black woman during a traffic stop when they mistakenly mistook her cellphone for a gun. Ingrid Mitchell, the black woman killed was on her way home after picking up her children from daycare when she encountered police.

Her eight-year-old son was shot in the leg during that incident. Later on that day when people were gathering in the black community to protest the killing of the unarmed black woman, and the injuring of her son, several police cars arrived to monitor the assembly, to make sure there were no disturbances or destruction of property.

The husband of the woman who just been killed was crying so hard it was sad. He was so weak with grief he could barely stand, and several men had to support him.

A lot of people were crying. The community was overwhelmingly shocked.

Most couldn't believe or understand how something like this could happen in their community. It seemed unreal.

Seeing it on TV or reading about it in the newspapers was totally different from the actual reality.

The pain – you could feel it in your chest, and it touched everyone around you.

The anger. The frustration. The sorrow. It was all real now.

And there was no one to turn to for help. As the community were mourning the loss of a loved one, a black pickup truck pulled up and came to a screeching halt in front of four police cars that were parked on the shoulder of the road.

Five men wearing red and blue bandanas over their faces jumped out of the truck.

They all had AK-47 assault rifles in their hands. There wasn't a single moment of hesitation. Immediately they opened fire and began spraying the police cars with bullets. The driver of the truck jumped out of the cab with a pump shotgun that had a drum attached to it and started blasting. The roar of gunfire and shell casings hitting the pavement were the only notable sound that could be heard for several moments. People were running and ducking, trying to take cover anywhere they could. The police were so overwhelmed they never had a chance to return fire. Women were screaming.

In all, six cops were killed. A seventh was left brain dead. They had to airlift him. He stayed on life support a year before they finally pulled the plug.

When the cops came knocking, asking people if they saw or heard anything, everyone clamed up. Most people slammed the door in their face. A couple of young thugs saw a crackhead snitch named Sammy talking to the police. They found Sammy the next day in a dumpster with half of his head blown off and a dead rat tide to his tongue . . . .

Four and a half hours later a black man, whose hands were cuffed behind his back, and wearing shackles, was beaten to death by guards at a prison in Raleigh, North Carolina. The prison had been notorious for brutalizing inmates for decades.

The next day around 7:00 PM during shift change when more than one hundred guards and staff members were exiting the building, two carloads of men and women pulled up and opened fire on the group, killing forty-one officers and staff members, and wounding eighteen more. It was the greatest loss of life prison officials had ever experienced since the prison was built more than one-hundred years ago.

Violent attacks against the criminal justice system became more and more rare as people took the fight to who they believed were the arch oppressors for centuries.

Chapter 24

Insurgency

Police all over the country believe that an organized criminal gang is responsible for the recent attacks that have occurred against law enforcement and public officials in the United States over the past several months.

"Multiple federal agencies are grossly involved in efforts designed to track down the leaders of this gang and bring them to justice. Every police department in the country has pledged their unwavering support in fighting against this unknown gang, who they have labeled as some type of domestic terrorist group.

"Many conservatives and their supporters are blaming the Black Lives Matter Social Justice Movement for these attacks.

"Dozens of Black Lives Matter Representatives have been receiving death threats from known White Supremist Groups and their prominent associates.

"Currently, Facebook and Google have banned the sites of these groups indefinitely due to a rise of daily posts of hate messages. According to –"

"See, that's the type of shit I'm talking about right there – these crackers talk about everything else, but they won't say a

Goddamn thing about these muthahfuckahs that's killing us. That shit be pissing me off," Andrew said, frowning.

"You ain't the only one," Trayvon replied.

"Trust me, these muthahfuckahs already know what time it is you feel me? They know exactly why they killing us it's all good; but now that niggahs is turning up, they wantah holler. . . Don't cry now muthahfuckahs," George said.

"You see how they killed that lady and shot her eight-year-old son? That shit was crazy," Breonna said.

"I know, right," Eric replied.

"Now what's really crazy is how them niggahs pulled up in that truck looking like the lynch mob," Fred said.

"Real talk."

"Mu-fuckahs still thinking shit sweet."

"Ah-fool!"

"You feel me?"

"I bet you we got their attention now," Trayvon said.

"There's no question about it."

"Ain't no fun when the rabbit got the gun," Eric said.

"Word-up."

Can the situation possibly get any worse? The Willie Lynch Curse was slowly lifting and there was no one on earth that could stop this revelation.

The phenomenon slave masters always spoke about and feared was finally upon them. The day that their former salves would turn against them had come.

The continuation of hate, discrimination and racism executed by the children of the former slave masters triggered the beginning of extraordinary colossal events that shattered the frame of America's democracy.

The Biden Administration suggested that the country should invest in the formation of a National Police Force.

The black community disregarded the President's comments as just more of the same, and nothing more than a make-over of the present criminal justice system's structure.

Many black leaders claimed that a National Police Force would mean more National Prisons and National Jails for the black and brown communities, and an even more militarized police force.

Republicans accused the President of being too soft on protesters and they begin to pass more and more harsh laws.

Jessie Helms, an openly racist State Senator from North Carolina was one of the main organizers bent on passing as many of these hateful laws as he could. He was an evil old bastard, known for always whistling Dixie in the presence of black people.

After leaving his office one day he went to his care, getting ready to go home, opened his car door and a bomb planted underneath his car exploded.

They found his legs across the street and the other half of his body on top of the State Capital Building.

Ole Jessie would never pass another hateful law in his life.

Especially not in this world.

Black Vigilantes.

The Executioner. That XAH QSHUNAH

Police in Compton California shot and killed an unarmed black man when an anonymous caller reported that an unknown suspect was breaking into someone's car.

When police arrived on the scene they encountered Tommy Lee Rutledge rambling inside of a vehicle which turned out to be his grandmothers. As Tommy Lee was exiting the car, police surrounded him and ordered him to freeze. Startled, Tommy Lee turned around and was shot multiple times in the chest. He died at the scene. Officers claimed that when Tommy Lee turned around he appeared to have a weapon in his hand. The so called weapon was actually his grandmother's car keys.

Two days later, the district attorney's office cleared officers of any wrongdoing and labeled the incident a justifiable homicide.

The entire city of Compton was in a total uproar and the unrest spread quickly thought the state. Men and boys, and some women, banded together and they armed themselves in different black communities all through the state and almost simultaneously they began to engage the police every time they entered a black neighborhood. In less than twenty-four hours more than a hundred police were killed and at least three hundred were injured.

Dozens of people were also killed by police which included an unofficial account of total injuries.

The National Guard was deployed and as of now the entire state of California is under lockdown.

State officials have declared a State of Emergency and are now in session discussing the possibility of invoking martial law.

Law enforcement agencies are blaming street gangs for the current uprising, and they've begun a nationwide crackdown against gang members. President Biden and Vice President Harris have condemned the violence and have pleaded for calm. The President and Vice President are calling on black leaders all over the country to participate in helping to quell the violence. Enormous protest and demonstrations against police violence have more than tripled over the past twenty-four hours.

China and several other world leaders have condemned the United States in support of Black Lives Matter.

Many officials are calling this the worst event ever in the history of America concerning social unrest.

CHAPTER 25

IT WAS THE MOMENT I FEARED

Everybody in America was glued to their TVs and iPhones, watching what was happening in California. Every news station in the country was broadcasting the uprising.

There were graphic images being shown of black men standing in the middle of the street with fully automatic machine guns, engaged in fierce gun battles with police all over the state.

Scenes of burnt out and over-turned police vehicles littering the streets and the smoking ruins of police buildings were horrifying.

"Dem niggahs don turnt all the way the fuck up!"

"You feel me!"

"Yo, look at Oh-Boy right there, that niggah dumpin on they ass," Eric said, pointing at the TV screen.

A chilling moment in history had arrived. In a painfully ironic twist, the oppressed had taken an aggressive stance in response to yet another police killing.

"I told y'all this shit was gonah pop, didn't I? . . . These muthahfuckahs just don't know when to quit. Now look at em .

. . Bitch ass muthahfuckahs calling the National Guard for help again," George said.

"This what they wanted ain't it?," Andrew said.

"Had to. . . they just looking for a reason to start openly killing us," Fred said.

"They're already openly killing us," Breonna said.

"That's all fact!," Eric said.

"Well it's been a long time coming, but niggahs definitely ready to ride now. You feel me?," Trayvon said.

"No doubt."

"Word up."

The chain of events unfolding seemed so unreal. But due to the continuation of centuries of hate, discrimination and racism, a once stable country was now whirling out of control.

"I think these muthahfuckahs believe that just because they're one of the military mights of the world, that muthahfuckas supposed to just sit by ideally and allow them to slaughter them."

"Shit, if that's what they think, they got another thing coming," Andrew said.

"You feel me yo? . . . I believe that's exactly what them miserable bastards be thinking." Eric said.

"Well I hate to be the one to buss they fuckin bubble, but if they actually believe in their cold hearts that they're going to silently lead us to the ovens like they did the Jews, then they might as well get ready for warfare, cause we bout to turn all the way the fuck up in this bitch, you feel me," George said.

"Big facts."

"Word-up!"

"Ride till I die!"

"As a matter of fact, it's time for us to cop those things from the Mexican so we can give our brothers and sisters in California a little bit of moral support, yah heard."

"Let's do this."

Meanwhile in Los Angeles, police were under heavy pressure, and were forced to regroup. They'd just experienced a part of policing that they'd never witnessed before. It was like some Black

Hawk Down shit all over again, where it seemed like every niggah in every black and brown community was shooting at them.

They were shocked.

This wasn't like a practical encounter with a suspect at a traffic stop or serving a warrant. This was straight out war. The reality of the situation was overwhelming. This was something the police were definitely not used to. Whereas blacks and Latinos were. Being targeted and killed because of the color of your skin wasn't a pleasant way to live at all.

But now, the shoe was on the other foot. Those who were oppressed now hunted the oppressor, and they've now discovered that they're vulnerable, and not the invincible superheroes they pretend to be.

They're human, they bleed, and they die just like any other creature God created.

Don't be led by a false intuition or blinded by the artificial myth that you will never be free; because in all actuality once you decide that you will no longer be the oppressed you will no longer be oppressed.

You'll be free.

CHAPTER 26

ACTIVE SHOOTER

George was admiring the high-powered assault rifle sitting on the tripod in front of him. Truly it was a work of art. It looked like something straight out of a Terminator movie. The design was absolutely sinister. He picked the weapon up and tested the weight of it. It was heavy. He liked the way it felt in his hands. George placed this eye to the high-powered scope attached to the rifle and immediately an infrared beam was activated.

"What the fuck is this?" George asked as he pointed the weapon at no particular object.

"As a matter of fact that's a good question," Trayvon said, "When I saw the shit I didn't even ask what was the name of it, I just said, let me get that."

"That shit look like that shit Megatron be shootin on Transformers," Eric said smiling.

"Word-up."

"Real talk."

"That damn thang taller than me," Breonna said, running her fingers over the weapon.

"These the bullets that came with it. It also got a silencer that you can attach to it. Dude said the bullets got nitroglycerin tips," Trayvon said.

"What's that?" Breonna asked, as she lifted one of the long bullets and studied it.

"It means after it hits something it'll explode on contact."

"I ain't never seen no bullet this big, it look like ah dick," she said.

"Well don't let me catch you playing with yourself with one of those things. I'd hate to see one of those things go off inside you," Eric said grinning.

"You ah real funny dude Eric," Breonna said rolling her eyes at him, and giving him a very mean look.

"How much did he charge you for this?" George asked as he continued to make his observations.

"Five thousand dollars. He let me have three of them for twelve," Trayvon said, "They got a one and three-quarter mile range also." He said.

"That's what you call long distance," Fred said.

"I know right."

"It's well worth it, if you ask me," Andrew said.

"That's a fact!" Eric Agreed.

"When you gonah test it out?" Fred asked.

"In the next couple of days," George said. "I hate to leave this beautiful muthahfuckah behind but it's just so damn big," George said.

"I know right, but we really don't got no choice. . . But it's all good tho, it'll serve it's purpose," Andrew said.

"True that."

"Maybe you can hide it and go back and get it," Breonna said.

"Niiiah, that's too risky. We'll just stick to doing what we been doing, you feel me," George said.

Everybody nodded their head in agreement.

"What else did you get?" Andrew asked.

Trayvon smiled, "A few more army guns and enough C-4 to blow up the world."

George spent the next two days scoping out his target and planning his position. It was time to bring the fight to the enemy once again.

A message was being sent. And it was plain and simple – stop killing us or else.

Peaceful protest – the slave master had no respect for it. It went in one ear and out the other. When we came with peace, the slave master comes with tear-gas and rubber bullets.

When we ask for justice, we get Selma. How long have we marched?

How long have we begged and pleaded to be treated like human beings?

We forgave the slave master and his children for all they've done to us, but yet, they continue to look upon us with scorn. Mercy, we cried.

But there was no mercy to be found.

We'll do anything to make you happy, we agreed. But the only thing that seemed to make them happy was our misery and our pain.

We have no more options left.

Truly, they meant to oppress us forever.

They are a vampiric race. They enjoy only the taste of our blood.

Do we continue to give our blood to them freely and let them drink until we're non-existent?

Or do we make them fight for it and leave a bitter taste in their mouths?

The sheep you slaughter are actually wolves in sheep's clothing, but you didn't take notice until they bare their fangs.

Black Vigilantes.

The Executioner . . .

George looked through the scope for the third time. He took a deep breath. He was ready. The scope he was using was so advanced that it digitally registered how far away you were from your target. It was amazing. It also had a button where you could turn the infrared beam on and off.

He was a little bit over a mile and a half away from the Durham Police Department, looking through the scope from a window in an old, abandoned building. It was the perfect setup.

Breonna was parked nearby waiting for his signal. It was 12:29 AM.

George picked up the silencer and screwed it onto the barrel of the assault rifle. He placed his eye to the scope again, scanning the police parking lot. He saw two officers in the parking lot talking. He waited.

Less than five minutes later seven more officers entered the parking lot. This was the opportunity he'd been waiting for.

George turned the infrared beam on and stuck his eye to the scope. He took aim. One of the officers was walking to his car when George leveled the gun and saw the little red dot appear on the back of the cop's head. He held his breath. Adrenaline began to flow through his veins. He welcomed it.

When the cop placed his keys in the lock to open the door to his vehicle, George pulled the trigger and watched as the cop's head literally exploded. The other officers hadn't even noticed yet that one of their fellow officers was down. George was already moving on to the next target. He took the second officer in the chest and watched him fly over the hood of an unmarked police car. By that time the other officers noticed that something was wrong. They drew their weapons and tried to take cover as they looked around and tried to figure out who was shooting at them and where the shots were coming from. Unknowingly they took cover right in the middle of George's crosshairs as he continued to pull the trigger, striking target after target, over and over.

George placed the beam on a cop's neck and pulled the trigger. The impact of the bullet ripped through the cop's neck, exploded and blew out a huge portion of his spine. In all, six cops were left dead. Another cop crawled up under a police vehicle, which is why he lived to tell about it.

Seconds after he'd fired his last shot George was already exiting the abandoned building and climbing into the car beside Breonna, who immediately drove off.

They were both dressed and had changed their appearance to look like old people. It didn't take long before they were on the freeway heading back to Rocky Mount.

"How did it go?" Breonna asked once they were miles away from the crime scene.

"Tell California we send our love and respects," he said, smiling.

Breonna leaned over and kissed him hard on the lips.

"I got something for you when we get back," she said with lust in her eyes.

"What is it?" George asked knowingly.

"All I can tell you is that it's hot and wet."

"How hot, and how wet?"

"Real hot, and real wet."

"Is that so?"

"Uhuh-huh."

"I like the sound of that," he said.

"I was hoping you would," she replied.

George began to think about what he was going to do to her, and an erection began to form. At the same time Breonna was thinking about what she wanted him to do to her and her panties became moist.

After dropping the car off that they used in Jackson, North Carolina, they switched the license plates, got in Breonna's car, and finally made their way home.

And sure as hell, just like Breonna said, she had something hot and wet for him. Real hot, and real wet.

After cutting up their disguises and flushing them down the toilet, "Can I suck that dick?" she asked. Voice sounding so sexy and sweet. George just smiled as she began digging her little hand inside his boxers.

Breonna was completely focused on her task and refused to be deterred. The throbbing between her legs begged to be beaten into submission.

Pulling the huge dick from his boxers, Breonna got down on her knees. She smiled. The sight of him always pleased her and made her pussy walls begin to melt. She admired the dick for a moment, as she stroked and played with it in her hand.

She could feel its pulse like a steady heartbeat. She drew closer. She rubbed the dick slowly against her face, running her soft lips gently over his length.

George groaned in the back of his throat with anticipation and pleasure.

Breonna smiled as she slowly began to caress his staff with tender kisses. Raising the shaft, she licked his balls, slowly, working her way up to the tip of his dick, then slowly working her way back down. Suddenly she became more aggressive as she plunged the huge chunk of meat in her mouth and began repeatedly forcing the dick down her throat.

"Uaugh! . . . . Uagh . . . . Aiiiah!," George groaned every time he felt the head of his dick slam into her throat. Back and forth, back and forth, back and forth, Breonna continued to gorge herself on the delicious black snake.

Pulling the dick from her mouth she began to lick the head of it like it was her favorite ice cream cone in the world. She was enjoying herself. She smiled again. She moaned. She squealed. She looked up. George was watching her closely. She looked into his eyes. The lust was unmistakable.

Still looking into his eyes Breonna placed the dick back between her lips and began riding him with her mouth once again. Putting both of her hands on his ass, she began pulling him repeatedly into her throat. She made a choking sound every time she pulled him towards her. And she still had her eyes locked on his.

George was in a trance as he swayed back and forth to her rhythm. Several times he had to steady himself. The pleasure she was giving him was truly overwhelming. Indeed this was one hell of a woman.

Breonna knew that if she kept the pressure on him much longer he would explode, and she didn't want that to happen.

At least not yet, anyway.

Slowly she pulled back releasing him from her mouth.

A long line of spit stretched from the tip of his dick and dripped from her luscious lips. Breonna licked her lips. She stood up and pulled off her panties and bra. She was now completely naked. She was ready.

Grabbing her around the thighs, George lifted her in the air. Breonna locked her legs around him.

Reaching behind herself she found the huge dick which she guided into the soft folds of her pussy lips. She felt the head break the opening of her cunt lips. It was inside her. Leaning back slightly without warning George dropped her onto his huge stump. Breonna screamed in pleasure, mixed with a little pain.

"Iaaaaaaaiiiiah!, stoop!," she cried when she felt the huge dick split her cunt lips apart and smash deeply within her walls. George lifted her again then dropped her onto his shaft.

"Ooooh!. . . Please! . . . Wait! . . . I- . . . Ooooh!," she continued to cry in pleasure, as George lifted her, then dropped her, lifted her, then dropped her, lifted her, and dropped her, again and again and again.

"Oooh Baby . . . . Oh God this dick so good," she moaned, "Ooooh Yeees! . . . . . Fuck me . . . Fuck me . . ," she cried.

"You like that baby? . . . . You want some more. . . Huh! . . . . Huh!," George said.

"Yeeeees," she replied in that sweet womanly voice.

George carried her to his bedroom. He continued to lift her up and drop her onto his sword as he carried her through the house.

Once he finally reached the bed he fell on top of her.

"Iaaaiiiah! Stooop!," she cried when she felt the dick go even deeper, hitting one of her most sensitive walls.

George began to dig and grind in the pussy. Her pleas and cries excited him even more. Aggressively he rolled her over onto her stomach. Her luscious, big juicy ass swayed in kind with every motion. He'd never had a woman with an ass so soft. It was a wonderful sight to see.

He didn't waste no time climbing on top of her and splitting her cunt lips in half with his shaft.

"Iaaaiiiah!" she cried when George brought all his weight down on her.

He began to rise and fall on her forcefully, plunging his member to the hilt every time he came down.

He grinded his hips, kissing the back of her neck while he whispered very nasty things in her ear.

Breonna gripped the bed sheets while trying to use a pillow to muffle her cries. She was drunk on pleasure. After experiencing her fourth orgasm in the bathroom she couldn't keep up with the count anymore.

Suddenly Breonna felt George pull his rod from her honey dip. She moaned in protest. The dick was quickly replaced by a hot little tongue wiggling around inside of her cunt hole. Breonna began to giggle with pleasure, as the soft tongue tickled her. She could feel another orgasm building inside of her. She welcomed it. It was calling her. She wanted it. Just when it was almost there, and she was about to cum again, George flipped her over onto her back, pinning her tiny feet over her head as he pushed her legs back. He pressed his lips to her pussy hole and sucked on her middle real hard.

"Iaaaiiiah!. . . Ooooh God!," she cried out when his hot mouth engulfed her entire pussy. Immediately she began to buck and shake as she climaxed, painting his tongue and lips with her fucking cream. She'd never came so hard in her life.

George continued to drink her love juices as Breonna climaxed over and over again. It was only the beginning of a long night of love making.

"Lick that pussy! . . . . lick that pussy . . . . Oooh God yeees!," she cried as she continued to shake and tremble.

The intensity of their sex increased. Whenever Breonna thought that she couldn't possibly go any higher George always seemed to amaze her by taking her to yet another level of extreme pleasure.

He dug in the pussy. He pulled it apart. He rubbed it. He pinched it gently. He pulled on it. And every time he touched her, her body screamed for more and more.

George stabbed the tip of his tongue into the crack of her asshole and a powerful orgasm shook her entire body. She got tongue tied. For a split second she couldn't remember her name or where she lived. She was totally fucked-up.

"Ooooh!," she cried as she squeezed the bed sheets tightly in her fist. George pushed his tongue a little deeper into her asshole and she nearly lost her mind.

He still had her legs pinned back, literally fucking her to death. No man in this world had ever made love to her like this, she was sure. He did things to her that caused her panties to get wet every time she thought about it.

Truly he was the most wonderful man she'd ever had.

Even though they'd known each other since they were kids, she now wished that she'd given him the pussy a long time ago.

Lost in her thoughts, she was brought back to reality when she felt herself being flipped over onto her stomach again. She had just enough time to catch a glimpse of his hardness and it looked even bigger for some reason.

Raising her onto her knees, George put the head of his poker into the opening of her slippery passage and slammed forward, splitting her cunt lips apart like hot butter.

"Iaaaiah! Stooop! . . . that's too much!," she cried. "Ooooh! . . . Nooo! . . . . . . Just be nice, ok please . . . . Ooooh! . . . Ooooh! . . . Oh God! . . . . . . Yeeeess," she moaned.

George held on tightly to her hips as he plunged into her repeatedly, slow and deep. Her womanly cries and pleas sounded so overwhelmingly loving and sweet that it finally took him over the edge, and he couldn't hold back any longer.

Grunting, jerking and twitching, George splattered her silky walls with his seed as he collapsed on top of her exhausted.

It was another night to remember.

CHAPTER 27

OFFICERS DOWN

We have to find out who did this, and we have to make them pay. More and more cops are getting killed every day and something has to be done about it! Somebody has to be held responsible and I really don't care who it is. . . The Chief wants answers or a lot of heads are going to roll," said Sergeant Miller Cox, a homicide detective for the Durham Police Department.

"Hell, we're already busting our balls on this case. These people seemed to be a lot smarter than we think. I'm beginning to believe that we might be dealing with experts," head homicide detective Captain Joe Mercer said.

"I don't give a fuck who they are. Once we find them they're toast!" Miller said banging his fist on the hood of their unmarked police vehicle.

"I agree. There won't be any of that 'you have the right to remain silent' bullshit."

The crime scene was crawling with cops and emergency personnel. Several news vans lined the streets, and a large crowd had gathered. A sniper with an extremely high-powered weapon had apparently ambushed about half a dozen police officers, killing five of them within minutes of the attack. There was blood everywhere.

Several onlookers in the crowd began to cheer, which started a commotion, causing multiple officers to have to be restrained.

It was a nightmare, which left the police wondering, "Who in the hell could be bold enough to try something like this?" A lot of cops were shaken up from the incident. Many of them that were up for retirement took it, while some just simply resigned. Everybody was aware of what was happening in California, and they knew why. Blacks were tired of being killed by police and they were retaliating.

"Hey Joe, come take a look at this will yah?" Miller said, waving him over.

"What's up?"

"Look at this . . . the bullet he was shot with went in here," Miller said pointing to the dead officers neck, "but look what it looks like when it came out here," he said pointing to the dead officer's head.

"It takes a very large bullet to do something like that . . . Last time I seen a man with a hole in him like that was when we were in Iraq."

"Jesus Joe, we got to catch these muthahfuckahs. They making us look bad."

"I couldn't agree with you more."

The situation in California had finally calmed down, but the overall tension between police and the black communities was still there. Helicopters and army Humvees were on frequent patrols throughout the state. Law enforcement remained on high alert for any possible disturbances, as state officials pleaded with all residents to remain calm.

A moment in American history had arrived that was long overdue.

Those who had been brutalized and killed by the police for centuries refused to tolerate it any longer. The tide had finally changed. For all of the authorities' misdeeds, there would be a swift reaction from the people.

Distraught with the uncontrolled and irresponsible power of those in charge, the public has shaken the very foundation of justice itself. For what form of law can be given to communities in which corruption has penetrated at every level?

Evil rules be advised, the holy function of the Lord's anointed has fallen from the King's head in the eyes of the people forever.

New World Order! The battle cry for those who persist to bring down the oppressor's high towers.

Altogether; We rise!

All over the country, black and brown communities were coming together like never before. The urgent need for a radically new world and the emancipation of all humanity was now evident. There were protests and rallies being held every day.

Who in the hell thought the revolution would be not be televised?

Not only was it being televised, but it was being broadcasted all over the world. Racism was once again on Front Street, and its evil methods of fear and control were now continually in question before the people. The root causes of hate and discrimination were being closely studied, while dialogue on the particular subjects increased.

But those same wicked men and women who believed that they were capable of making America great again through the use of violence and terror refused to be swayed by those they felt threatened their power.

Shortly after dawn on June 19th, 2020, a group of White Nationalists stormed a Black Lives Matter rally in Washington County, Minnesota, where protesters were demanding that murder charges be brought against a Brooklyn Center policewoman for fatally shooting an unarmed black man in the chest during a routine traffic stop.

While protesters were gathered in the street outside the home of the Washington County District Attorney, a minivan containing seven men and two women plowed into the crowd of protesters killing three and injuring six more.

Seconds after the collision the seven men and two women, all armed with AR-15 assault rifles, exited the minivan and immediately began indiscriminately shooting into the crowd of protesters.

Screams of panic ensued as people began to run for their lives. Many protesters were trampled to death as the fleeing crowds scrambled for safety and cover.

Several witnesses to the incident claimed that police stood by idly as the attackers continued to mow down the crowd of fleeing protesters. Fifty-one people were killed, including fourteen children. More than two dozen were injured.

Dead bodies littered the street as if a tornado had swept through the area, causing chaos and destruction.

Filing back into the minivan, the attackers fled the scene. The police did not pursue them.

Video footage from phones and police cruisers and body cams captured the entire incident. Cries of agony and sorrow could be heard as women clutched the lifeless bodies of their child or loved one in their arms.

The pain and suffering of the horrifying event were overwhelmingly heart wrenching and unbearable. Nearly all the protesters had been shot in the back while trying to escape the carnage according to police reports.

Sirens could be heard in the background as emergency vehicles made their way to the scene.

Many survivors of the attack began loading those that were injured into their cars and rushing them to the hospital.

It was a nightmare.

The black community was shocked by the event, but not surprised at all. The same tactics used by hateful men and women for centuries was very much still alive. It was just another chapter of America's long dark history exposing itself once again. A list of atrocities which never seem to end.

Two days after the mass shooting, the seven men and two women that carried out the attack were identified and arrested. Three retired police officers, two Navy veterans, one active-duty police Sergeant and three known members of a local militia were positively identified and charged with multiple counts of murder and attempted murder, and assault with a deadly weapon with intent to kill inflicting serious injuries.

The discovery of police involvement in the attacks sparked a mass demonstration outside the Brooklyn Center Police Department.

Police in riot gear responded with tear gas and rubber bullets as demonstrators threw rocks and Molotov cocktails.

Dozens of protesters were arrested as they clashed with police. By nightfall, many parts of the city were on fire.

City officials along with the mayor issued an immediate curfew, while business owners called on the governor to deploy the National Guard. Law enforcement agencies across the state braced themselves for possible violence as the President ordered the Department of Justice to launch a special investigation into the practices of the Brooklyn Center Police Department.

The incident caused an uproar throughout the country. Tensions between police and black and brown communities increased dramatically. Radical black groups called on the people to arm and protect themselves, and not to be afraid to die for their God-given right to be treated as human beings.

Passive black leaders warned that violence wasn't the way to achieve progress in fighting against social injustice and that the people needed to remain calm.

One black preacher who suggested that defunding the police wasn't a good idea for the black community was later found dead, dangling from his pulpit by his suspenders.

The revolution will be televised.

A month and a half after the Minnesota shooting rampage, retired Navy SEAL, Fred Hampton had finally finished construction of the massive bomb he'd been building. It was a mixture of all kinds of explosive materials that he had steadily accumulated. He was a very sad and angry man, who now saw the world as a living hell.

After the killing of his daughter and sixteen-year-old grandson at the Social Justice rally a month and a half ago, he had lost all faith in America.

He remembered how his father used to always tell him that if he worked hard and lived a law-abiding life that everything would be fine, and that even though hate and racism was an issue in the country he would be able to overcome it.

Fred trusted and believed his father, and he'd done everything in his power to do what he said, but somehow it still wasn't enough for him to keep his family safe. He'd worked his ass off to provide for his family and serve his country, but the same country he'd tried to love and protect came back and took everything away from him.

He was heartbroken and devastated. A sixty-eight year old man with nothing left but pain and memories.

Over and over he asked himself, how can the same people he fought with, and risked his life for, come back and kill his whole family? It was unbelievable.

Every night he laid down after drinking himself to sleep, and wished that when he woke up everything that happened would have just been a bad dream, and that his daughter and grandson would still be alive when he woke up. But every morning as soon as he opened his eyes he knew that the bad dream he'd hoped for was actually reality, and that he would never get the chance to touch his daughter or grandson again or tell them how much he loved them.

He became bitter. All the happiness and love that he'd known had been erased.

His only reason for living now was to bring suffering to those who had caused him such pain and grief. He plotted against them. The rage inside him was like lava spilling from an erupting volcano. Kill, kill, kill. That's all he could think of. The very depths of his soul had been consumed with an insane madness. He ran his hand through his gray hair. His armpits were wet with sweat. He didn't even realize that he was gritting his teeth until his cell phone rang.

"Yeah," Fred said, answering on the fourth ring.

"Hey Fred, this is Pastor Smith, praise the Lord, how are you?"

"Who?"

"Pastor Smith, from Oak Hill Baptist Church. Don't tell me you don forgot what church you belong to," the pastor said.

"Yeah, whatever, what do you want," Fred replied, agitated.

"I'm sorry. Are you alright? It's just that we haven't seen you in a while and we wanted to let you know that Jesus loves you and that we're praying for– "

"Man, I don't got time for that Jesus shit! Where the fuck was Jesus when them crackers was gunning my baby girl and my grandson down in the street?!"

"I'm sorry Fred, I can imagine the pain that you're in and we're going to pray for – "

"Preacher man, you couldn't possibly imagine the pain that I'm in so stop saying that. . . Tell me, was your family just murdered by a bunch of racist rednecks?" Fred asked as he began to shout.

"No Fred and I – "

"Well then, how in the fuck you gonah sit there and say that you know how I feel? I feel like shit! I feel like my whole world is destroyed because these hateful muthahfuckahs can't see past a person's skin color!" Fred was now screaming into the phone, gripping it so hard that the screen cracked.

"Forgive me Fred. We're gonah pray that the Lord – "

"Pray!! Pray to who?! You want me to get down on my knees and pray that a cracker with wings comes down out of the sky and makes everything better? Is that what you want me to do? Huh! I can't believe you niggahs still falling for the same shit them crackers used to enslave us with. Makes me sick to my stomach. As a matter of fact, I'd appreciate if you wouldn't call here no more. . . I tell you what, call me when Jesus comes back. I got a few questions I'd like to ask him," Fred hung up on him.

Fred continued to mumble to himself, "Stupid muthahfuckah calling here talking bout this holy-rollie ass shit. Kill these muthahfuckahs. Hateful sons of bitches." Fred walked back to his shed. He'd just thought of a few more components that he could add to the bomb.

When he pulled back the blanket to reveal the bomb that covered the entire bed of his truck, for the first time in more than a month Fred was smiling. He seemed happy.

But in all actuality, underneath the mask a trained eye would have noticed that Fred had totally lost his mind.

There was no question about it.

Exactly fifty-seven days after the Minnesota Social Justice Rally massacre, Fred Hampton was sitting in his truck in the parking lot of a Wal-Mart shopping center, two blocks away from the Brooklyn Center Police Department. It was three-thirty in the afternoon on a beautiful spring day. The sun was shining bright. A wonderful, relaxing warm breeze occasionally blew. The skies were clear as far as one could see.

Fred thought about his daughter and grandson. A teardrop fell from his eye, blurring his vision. He wiped it away. He checked his watch; it was now a little after four o'clock. Today was going to be a big day for the Brooklyn Center Police Department. The Mayor was holding a press conference and he'd invited several guests to join him. The Mayor and the City Council had taken a hard stance against defunding the police in his bid for re-election. According to the polls, he was currently leading his opponent by double digits, while new stations had already begun to predict him as the winner of the race.

Within forty-eight hours he was confident that he'd be sworn in and starting his third term as Mayor.

It was a lot of handshaking and smiling and plenty of pats on the back going on when the Mayor finally took the podium and began to address reporters and a large group of supporters.

"Ladies and Gentlemen, I'd like to thank y'all good folks for coming out on this fine day in Minnesota. I really appreciate all of you for supporting and trusting me to do what's best for our city and all the people that keep us safe. I mean, where would we be without law enforcement? Just ask yourself, what kind of society would we be? I know that there's been a lot of talk about defunding our outstanding police force, but I assure you that I'll do everything in my power to make sure that this doesn't happen. I wouldn't dare ask any of you good citizens to live in a place where you're not sure if someone is coming when you call for help. That's just not the way we do things around here. No sir-ree . . . I know that we might have a few problems but getting rid of the men and women who protect us is definitely not the answer."

The Mayor paused for a few seconds while the audience applauded. He smiled. Standing behind him, the Chief of Police, the Commissioner, the City Council and other prominent city officials also applauded.

"Thank you," the Mayor said, holding up his hand attempting to calm the crowd. He looked at his beautiful wife. He squeezed her hand. She squeezed his back giving him more support and encouragement. Their two wonderful children stood by her side.

"Thank you . . . Now I –"

Suddenly a black pick-up Dodge Ram truck jumped the curb traveling at about fifty miles per hour crashing through a line of reporters and spectators. Immediately police began to fire on the truck as it mowed through the crowd towards the Mayor who was standing on the steps of the Police Department. The panicked crowd began to scatter. Many people were already dead as the truck continued to barrel it's way forward.

Police continued to open fire, filling the cabin of the truck with dozens of holes. The Mayor, his family, the Chief of Police, the Commissioner and members of the City Council were all running for cover when a flash of light brighter than the sun illuminated the entire area. The ground shook as the heat from the powerful explosion burned up everything in its path. The shockwave could be felt for two miles away. The entire front section of the Brooklyn Center Police Department building turned into a pile of dust and twisted metal, and Fred Hampton and his truck was blown into a hundred million particles. They couldn't find enough pieces of him to bury.

The Mayor, the Chief of Police, the Commissioner and all the council members were all killed instantly. The Mayor's wife and two children were never found and were believed to have been evaporated. Everybody who attended the Mayor's press conference were dead.

Fifty-three police officers were killed in the initial blast, and eighty-nine more died when the bomb's radius reached the Brooklyn Center Police Department's building.

Every store front window for a half a block were all blown out. Many people suffered minor injuries from flying glass and debris.

A huge cloud of dust and smoke hung heavily in the air. The shrill of dozens of car alarm systems could be heard. Body parts of the victims were laying everywhere. Multiple cars were overturned and burning freely.

The sound of approaching emergency vehicles became louder.

Spectators began to film the destruction with their phones.

Within minutes, the world was describing the incident as a domestic terrorist attack.

No Justice.

No Peace.

CHAPTER 28

FRED HAMPTON

In our top headline for this evening, we'll now take you to the scene in Washington County, Minnesota where a suicide bombing attack has just taken place at the Brooklyn Center Police Department.

"According to our spokesperson, this vicious attack occurred during a press conference that was being held by the Mayor and other high ranking City Officials. The Mayor's family was also killed in the attack.

"Surveillance footage from police body cams and surrounding businesses show this man-would-be attacker, who police have identified as Fred Hampton, a retired Navy Chief, plowing his vehicle through a line of spectators and reporters, then detonating a bomb which caused a powerful explosion.

"As you can see, the magnitude of the bomb's destruction was devastating. More than three hundred people are believed to have died in this horrific attack. More than half were police officers.

"Apparently minutes before the attack, the would-be suspect posted a video claiming responsibility.

"The suspect blamed law enforcement for the killing of his daughter and grandson at a Social Justice Rally a little over a month ago, where gunmen opened fire on the crowd killing fifty-one protestors and injuring more than two-dozen. This tragic event is one of many that have law enforcement agencies all over the country highly concerned about the escalating rate of retaliatory attacks against authority figures.

"President Biden and Vice-President Harris condemned the attack and called it another senseless act of violence that will not be tolerated.

"The President and the Vice-President also sent their condolences to the families of the bombing victims and pledged their unwavering support. The President is also due to visit the site of this tragic event sometime tomorrow.

"After raiding the home of the suspect, investigators found an abundance of bomb making materials, which the suspect apparently used to construct the deadly device.

"Investigators also found more videos of the suspect recording himself as he made preparations for the bomb.

"So far investigators believe that the suspect acted alone, but according to other law enforcement sources the investigation is still ongoing." . . . .

Black Vigilantes.

THAH XAH QSHUNAH!

CHAPTER 29

BABY MOMMA

"Eric and Trayvon are in the hospital."

"Word-up, what happened?" George asked, looking very concerned.

"They caught Covid-19," Breonna said.

"Damn. That shit got the whole world fucked up."

"I know, right."

"Have you took the vaccine yet?," George asked.

"No, have you?"

"No. I want to, but I'm just a little paranoid. Crackers don experimented and created so much shit to try to kill us off that it's hard to trust anything they say," George said with a skeptical look on his face.

Breonna frowned, "I feel the same way. Especially after reading that book Black Holocaust. I'm scared."

"Me too. But we might not have no other choice. Anyway, I doubt if they'd put some shit out there that will kill of the entire population," George said.

"That's true, but what if it just only kills us?" Breonna replied looking unsure.

"You have a point."

"There's something I need to tell you too," Breonna said. She seemed a little hesitant.

"What's good?"

She took a deep breath. George could tell that she was a little nervous.

"What's up Bee? It's all good, don't worry, you can tell me anything babe." His soothing words calmed her nerves a little bit. She smiled.

"I'm going to have your baby," she said rubbing her hand over her midsection.

George's heart swelled with pride. He was overwhelmed with joy. He grabbed her, picked her up and started spinning her around. He was so happy.

"That's wonderful! That's the greatest news I've ever heard in my life," he said as he kissed her and continued to twirl her around. "God I love you so much Bee," he said smiling. He kissed her some more.

"I love you too," she said as he held her close.

"Why you act like you were scared to tell me that?" he asked.

"I don't know. With so much that's going on, I didn't think that you would want to have a child right now. I mean, due to the type of lifestyle that we're living it's obvious that nothing's promised."

"You're right. . . I don't know, maybe this is a sign that it's time for us to chill."

"It might be," she looked into his eyes hopefully.

George thought about it. There was no question that ah muthahfuckah couldn't say that him and his team hadn't put in their share of work to support the struggle; a true fact. He looked into her loving eyes. He firmly embraced her.

"What do you want, Bee?" he asked.

Breonna wrapped her arms around him even tighter, "I want us to be together. I want to have a life and a family together, and I'm willing to do anything to make that possible. I truly love you, more than I have any man. I've never experienced such complete happiness as this before and I want it to last forever. You're my man."

"I feel the same way about you."

"Do you?"

"You know I do."

She couldn't stop smiling. Her emotions were on maximum overdrive right now.

George was still excited by the fact that he was about to become a father as he openly admired her beautiful being.

"This calls for a celebration. I'm bout to roll up a blunt and smoke one to the head. I want you to grab that bottle of gin out the fridge and meet me in the bedroom . . . and Bee?"

"Yeah."

"Make sure when you get there you're not wearing any clothes."

She was smiling brightly as George walked away singing one of his favorite songs, "There's a meeting in my bedrooooooooom! Please don't be laaah, aaaa, aaate!"

Breonna took off running for that bottle of gin, snatching off her clothes as she went.

A few minutes later . . .

Breonna entered the bedroom with the bottle of Gin in her hand, ass naked. Pussy wet.

"Hey baby momma," George said smiling as he took a long pull of marijuana smoke into his lungs.

"Heeey," Breonna said returning his smile.

"Why don't you grab one of those cups over there and fill it up with some gin for me." Breonna did as she was told. George watched her. He couldn't take his eyes off her luscious ass. The way it moved when she walked was making his dick hard.

George was sitting on the edge of the bed. He was also naked.

Breonna walked over and handed him the tall cup of gin which he drained immediately. She couldn't take her eyes off the huge chunk of meat between his legs which seemed to get longer and longer every second. She wanted it. As a matter of fact she could almost taste the salty thang in her mouth. She reached for it. George smacked her hand away.

"Not so fast baby momma," George said shaking his finger at her, "I got to make sure you're ready before I give you some."

"See. Why you want'ah play now," she said sucking her teeth and folding her arms over her breasts. She rolled her eyes.

George smiled. She rolled her eyes again.

George climbed back onto the bed.

Breonna climbed onto the bed beside him.

"Come sit on my face. I'm going to stick my tongue out and I want you to ride it for a little while.

Breonna was already in motion before he could finish the sentence.

"Turn around. I want'ta play with your ass while you do it," he said.

Breonna turned around. George grabbed her luscious ass in both of his hands and pealed her cheeks open. He stuck his tongue out.

Slowly she lowered herself onto it.

"Ooooh! . . . God!," she cried, the little hot pink flesh cut through her middle.

She rose and came down slowly on that meaty little thang again, and a fire began to burn inside her.

"Unuuugh! . . . . . . Unuuuugh! . . . . . . Unuuuuaghah!" she moaned as she began to bounce up and down on his tongue.

A wave of pleasure coursed through her entire body. It felt like someone was pouring something warm all over her. She was filled with lust. Her first orgasm came and before she knew she was bucking and screaming, grinding her pussy onto his hot mouth and tongue.

"Suck this pussy! . . . . . Please suck this pussy! . . . Ohooo! Yeeeess!" she was enjoying herself. The sexy noises she was making sounded so sweet. Like music to his ears.

Holding her firmly, George sucked on the pussy real hard for several seconds, and she rewarded him by splattering his upper lip with a fresh coat of fuck cream. Greedily he lapped her nectar as she continued to literally melt on his hot, wanting tongue.

"Lick that pussy! . . . lick that pussy! . . . Ooooh! Lick that pussy good babe!" she cried.

George was pleased by her happiness. But here was yet still more to come. Rolling her off of him he stood up. He grabbed a tee-shirt and wiped his face. The Gin was starting to kick in. He filled his cup again and drained it.

Breonna watched him. She waited patiently. George climbed back onto the bed.

Breonna turned around quickly and got in the doggie style position, face down, ass up high. Reaching back, she pealed the ass and pussy open for him. He loved when she positioned herself for him like that. It made her look even more sexy.

He got behind her, stuck the head in, then rammed forward.

"Iaaaaiiiah! Stooooop!" she cried when she felt the long hard dick slam home.

"Don't cry now," George said playfully as he began to beat the pussy up royally. He held on to her hips tightly while he dug all in the pussy. He went slow. He went medium. He went fast. He climbed on her back. Licked and kissed on her neck. He made love. He was tender and caring. He fucked hard. He was rough and aggressive.

"Iaaaaiiah, yeeess! . . . Fuck me! . . . . . fuck me good . . . Fuck me good! . . . Ooooh! . . . Ooooh!" she cried as George tore the pussy up. She like what he was doing to her. He messed around and went a little too deep, "Ooooh! . . . . . . Nooooooo!," she screamed, "Please don't go so deeeeeep," she moaned and pleaded. She ran from the dick. She didn't get far. She was on her stomach, and he was on top of her giving her the business. He kissed her neck again. He sucked on it. She turned her head to the side, and he put his tongue down her throat. All the while continuing to dig the pussy out.

"Aaugh! . . . . Aaugh! . . . . . Iaaughah!" he groaned as he plowed into her silky tunnel. Aggressively George flipped her over onto her back. He placed her little feet over his shoulders.

He didn't waste any time sinking back into her slippery warmth. He buried himself inside her to the hilt, ramming his rod into one of her sensitive walls.

"Iaaaaiiiah, stooooop!" she cried when she felt him hit the bottom of the pussy. She was powerless to ward off his deep thrust in such a submissive position. She tried to bring her feet down from over his shoulders. George put'em back up there and continued to beat the pussy up. He worked it like a pro. Grinding the dick into her forcefully.

She had that look on her face like, "I am, getting, the shit, fucked out of me. Goddamn!"

If they wanted to, they probably could make their own sex tapes and get rich. George finally rolled off of her. He stood up. He poured himself another cup of gin. The first two cups already had him buzzin. Breonna watched him knowingly. He smiled as he took a huge gulp from his cup of gin.

"You trin tah kill me in here, ain't 'chah?," she said smiling.

"Why you say that, you ready for me to stop," he asked.

She shook her head, "no."

"Good. Now come over here and put your mouth on this dick and suck it like you love me. And bring a couple of pillows with you. I wouldn't want you to scrape those pretty knees up on the hardwood floor," George said, his words starting to slur.

Hurryiedly Breonna snatched two pillows off of the bed and walked over to where George was standing. Dropping the pillows at his feet, she fell to her knees. The dick was already hard and waiting for her. Resting both of her hands on her thighs, she stretched her neck forward and engulfed the head of the dick between her lips. She pulled back, making a loud popping sound with her mouth. She repeated the same process again, very slow and delicately.

George groaned as he watched her work her magic. Breonna smiled. She loved giving him pleasure. Stretching her neck forward again, she took more of the dick into her mouth. She could smell and taste a little of her cunt juices on him. She didn't mind, this was her baby daddy. The taste of her own pussy even excited her a little. It made her feel freaky. The lust inside her began to rise. Every time she plunged the dick in her mouth she added a few more inches to her depth. George was mesmerized. He couldn't take his eyes off of her sexy lips. Every time his dick disappeared into her face it felt like he was being eaten alive.

Placing her little hands on the back of his knees, Breonna began to plow the dick into her mouth greedily. She choked on it. She gagged. She didn't slow down or miss a beat as she continued to feast hungrily on the huge chunk of meat.

Back and forth. Back and forth. Back and forth. She sucked it slow. She sucked in up tempo. She sucked it hard and fast.

"Aaaaaaugh! . . . . Aaaaaaaaugh!," George groaned every time she came down on him. His knees were getting weak. His legs trembled. His body convulsed.

When Breonna began plunging the dick into her throat and making those choking sounds, George finally lost control. Before he realized what he was doing he had a hand full of her hair grunting and jerking as he repeatedly plunged his dick down her throat, spilling his seed until he was empty and exhausted. Even after he was spent, Breonna continued to lick and kiss on the head of his pole until she had drained him of every drop.

"Damn! Superhead ain't got shit on you Baby Momma," George said, smiling.

Breonna smiled back.

On wobbly legs George walked over to the dresser and poured himself another cup of gin. He drained his cup, then filled it up again.

Breonna gave him that look.

He smiled, "Gon get up there on the bed. I'll be ready in a few minutes. I want you to sit on it this time."

Breonna smiled.

CHAPTER 30

DEADLY VIRUS

I hope these muthahfuckahs don't shut us down again with all this Covid shit that's going on."

"Ain't no telling with these clowns, they basically do what they want'ah do."

"Ain't that the truth."

The barber shop was packed today. George came in, took a seat, and waited for his turn to get a haircut.

"Hey, George, what's shakin, fool," Mike Mike, one of the barbers said when he spotted George.

"Ain't shit, what's good with you Mike Mike? How's business?" George asked.

"I don't know about tomorrow, but it's damn sure looking good today, you feel me," Mike Mike smiled, showing a mouth full of gold teeth.

"That's what's up."

"Yo George, what's up?," Big Time, the other barber said.

The third barber, Old Man Sam threw George the black power sign.

"Yo, how y'all doin?," George replied.

All the barbers knew George. They liked him. He was a straight up real brother from around the way, and everybody respected him.

"I got two more heads in front of you George and I'll be right with you," Mike Mike said.

"Take your time bro, I'm not in a rush."

"I got you."

"Yo, y'all see what O'Boy did the other day in Minnesota? Dude was on some straight madman shit you feel me," Big Time said.

"Shit, you would be too if muthahfuckahs kilt your daughter and grandson."

"You better believe it."

"I told y'all, muthahfuckahs is tired of being killed by the white man. Now back in my time they was really getting away with that shit. But today it's ah whole new ball game. Them young boys grippin that iron," Old Man Sam said.

"Same shit with Michael Johnson, them niggahs ain't playing the radio no more."

"That's ah fact."

"These muthahfuckahs still stuck in the fifties and sixties ain't they?"

"I don't know, but niggahs sure sending they ass back to the future, you feel me." Mike Mike said.

"Ha, ha, ha, ha, ha."

George sat there and listened. He always loved to hear how they went back and forth in the barber shop. It was either sports or politics. All the time.

"Now dem boys down there in California showed their ass. police killed a unarmed black man down there and them niggahs shot up the whole fuckin state." Big Time said.

"Now back in my day they used to say that the revolution would not be televised but I'm not too sure about that now."

"It's crazy. This shit is poppin off everywhere. As soon as the police do some fucked up shit niggahs is ridin."

"And it's about damn time."

"Shit, every time something happen crackers wait to blame Black Lives Matter."

"I know right. But they don't never blame themselves. Every time you turn around they talking bout, we thought he had a gun. Oh, he was reaching for something."

"Don't forget about their latest one, 'I thought I was reaching for my taser.'"

"Bitch! You been with the police department twenty years, and you mean to tell me that all of a sudden you can't tell your gun from your taser. . . get the fuck out of here."

"Then you got muthahfuckahs like Tim Scott talking about 'America is not inherently racist.' These house niggahs kill me. As soon as they get that degree from Harvard or Yale they become whiter than the whitest white man."

"That's a fact!"

"That niggah Shelby Steele the same way."

"Who is that?"

"The niggah that made that movie What Killed Michael Brown."

"O yeah, I know who you talking about now."

"This house niggah uses every excuse in the world to downplay racism and he tries to compare the racism of our time with his in the sixties. He says that white guilt equals Black power. Can you believe this boot licker? Then he'll say some shit like, 'you might have a few incidents of racism here and there, but it's not everywhere.' Can you believe this clown? Somebody needs to tell this clown that if racism affects one of us it's affecting us all."

"I know that's right."

"This niggah always putting down the Black Lives Matter Movement. He be crying talking bout, 'Amazon gave Black Lives Matter ten million dollars, but they canceled my movie.' This fools the worst."

"Somebody need to tell that clown that Amazon might of gave him ten million dollars if he stood against racism like Black Lives Matter instead of trying to get the world to pretend like it don't exist."

"That's ah fact."

"Yo George, come on bro. You ready for me to hook you up?" Mike Mike said.

George got up and sat in the chair.

"It sure is a lot going on in America."

"You can say that again."

"Speaking of which, you know the Lakers don fucked around and picked up Westbrook?"

"Say word!"

"That's on everything."

"Bron, Bron, A.D., and Westbrook!, Lakers ah fool for that."

"Labron on his monopoly shit again."

"Word up."

"What about those Carolina Panthers?" Big Time said.

"Man, fuck the Panthers! Every time I bet on dem muthah-fuckahs I lose my money."

"Niggah, stop hatin!"

"Hatin! Hatin on what? Them muthahfuckahs is trash and you know it . . . Y'all muthahfuckahs always talking bout somebody hatin on something. Y'all niggahs kill me with that shit." Mike Mike said, frowning.

"Niggah who your team?! Every time I turn around you on another bandwagon. This niggah be jumpin ships like ah pirate in this muthahfuckah, Goddamn!" Big Time said.

"Damn sure do," Old Man Sam said shaking his head.

"Shut the fuck up Sam! . . . This old muthahfuckah be going for the Dallas Cowboys – he ain't been to Texas a day in his God-damn life!"

"Hell, at least I got ah team. You switch more teams than ah bitch shaking her ass. What's that song dem young boys be rap-pin, talkin bout. All muthahfuckah jumpin from dick to dick?," Old Man Sam said.

The whole barber shop was cracking up.

"Watch your mouth Sam," Mike Mike said. He had a smirk on his face.

Sam patted his pocket for the Hawk Bib he kept tucked away, just in case the young boy tried to get stupid.

After leaving the barber shop George drove to Breonna's apartment. When she answered the door he could tell that she'd been crying.

"What's wrong?" he asked, holding her in his arms. Breonna burst into tears again.

"Baby what's wrong?" George asked again, concerned.

"Erick died from Covid this morning. He—" she began crying again.

George was shocked by the news. It almost seemed unreal. The pandemic had finally reached their doorsteps and it had left a bloody footprint in its wake. None of them had really taken the pandemic serious enough. They'd basically chose to ignore it, which had proven to be a deadly mistake. Even though the virus had killed more than seven hundred thousand people in America alone, it seemed that the reality of that massive loss of life didn't affect ones consciousness until it actually hit home.

"Come on, let's go," George said, grabbing her by the hand.

"Where are we going?" she asked.

"To get vaccinated. I can't take the chance of losing you or my baby. It's too much of a risk. Eric would probably be alive right now if he'd gotten the shot. I don't want to be laying in some hospital bed a few weeks from now, clinging to my life, wishing I'd taken the shot when I had the chance."

"So basically we're forced to let Bill Gates and Doctor Fauci put that chip in our ass?" Breonna said with a smile on her face.

"Trust me, I know how you feel. I feel the same way. But what choice to we have? Now's definitely not the time to play games with our lives, wouldn't you agree?"

Breonna shook her head, "But I'm scared," she said, holding him tighter.

"Me too. But I'd rather be scared than dead, you feel me?"

"If you say so," she poked her lip out.

George kissed her. She kissed him back.

"Come on, let's go," he said.

"O.K., just let me grab my purse."

"Damn, this fuckin line long as hell. I see why people don't want to get the shot now," Breonna said, rolling her eyes and sucking her teeth.

"So you saying you'd rather wind up like Eric?" George said.

"Hump."

George was reading one of the flyers a nurse had given him while they waited to get their shots.

"What's that?" Breonna asked.

"Some information about Covid."

"What it say?"

"You want me to read it to you?"

"Yeah."

"It says Coronavirus disease, Covid-19 is spreading at an alarming rate across the United States. The new Delta variant, one of many mutations of the original disease, is highly contagious, and it is infecting people, especially those who have not been vaccinated. Right now tens of thousands of people are hospitalized across the country, and hundreds are dying every day. Nearly all Coronavirus deaths are among people who have not been vaccinated – over forty-one percent of people in this country who are eligible over twelve years old have not been fully vaccinated.

"In the United States, where the vaccine has been available to most eligible people, an important part of why people are not getting the vaccine is confusion, disinformation and misinformation, and a campaign of lies about the vaccine itself, how it works, and why it is important to take it.

"According to the World Health Organization; germs are all around us, both in our environment and in our bodies. When a person is susceptible and they encounter a harmful organism, it can lead to disease and death. When a pathogen does infect the body, our body's defenses, called the immune system, are triggered and the pathogen is attacked and destroyed or overcome.

"When the pathogen is a disease-causing organism the body has never encountered before, it takes time for the immune system to recognize it, and to produce ways to defeat it. One of the most important parts of the body's defenses are called antibodies – large proteins that are able to recognize pathogens and neutralize them so they cannot infect the body.

"Vaccines have been developed over hundreds of years and have saved untold millions of lives all across the world. What vaccines do is provoke an antibody-response – they train the body to recognize the pathogen and develop the antibodies to defeat it before the pathogen arrives. Some vaccines contain weakened or inactive parts of a pathogen which provoke the body to produce antibodies. Newer vaccines contain the 'blueprint for producing antibodies.' Regardless of what kind of vaccine, it will not cause the disease in the person receiving the vaccine, but it will train the immune system to be able to mobilize against the disease. The –"

"Dang, you gonnah read the whole book aint'chah? I get it already," Breonna said rolling her eyes and sucking her teeth again.

George laughed.

She looked even more beautiful when she was upset.

"Man, my feet hurt," she said putting her hands on her hips, shifting from foot to foot.

"Shit, if I had to haul that much ass around every day my feet would probably hurt all the time too," George said, grinning.

Breonna punched him in the ribs, "I see you got some jokes you wantah share. Huh? . . . Well if I was toting around what you're carrying I'd probably have chronic back pains, duhah," she said rolling her eyes and twisting her neck in that womanly way.

George couldn't stop laughing. "I tell you what – when we get back I'll rub your feet for long as you want. How does that sound Baby Momma?" he said, pulling her close.

"I'd rather you rubbed on something else if you don't mind," she said mischievously.

"I don't know, depends on what it is," George said knowingly.

"Do you want me to yell it out?"

"Naw! How bout you whisper it in my ear," he said.

Breonna stood on her tiptoes. George leaned forward. She cupped his right ear and whispered, "this fat juicy pussy."

"Oooooh, you so nasty."

Breonna was smiling wickedly.

The line was starting to get shorter, finally, even though they'd been standing in it for nearly an hour.

"I've been thinking about something too," George said.

"What's that?" she replied.

"Us moving in together."

"That might be a good thing . . . I like the sound of that. I wouldn't mind waking up to you every morning," she said, wrapping her arm around his waist.

"I'd love waking up to you, Baby Momma," George said squeezing her tight.

"When you want to do it?"

"Today."

"You don't waste no time do you?" she said smiling.

"Why?"

She smiled again. She was in love, no doubt about it.

He was too.

They shared a dangerously dark secret. So dark, that it could never be told.

They'd made a daring attempt and they'd gotten away with it.

They'd gotten away with murder. Murders that would make them wanted men for life. Like so many others before them, they'd taken the fight to their enemies. The enemy of the people.

It was a constant battle between the oppressed and a centuries old oppression that never seemed to end. All because a core group of evil racist men and women refused to embrace peace and true justice for all.

George knew this. Even though he loved Breonna with all his heart, he knew also that he would never turn his back on his people as long as the fight for true freedom continued. It wasn't about them. it was about a collective group of people that had suffered for far too long. It was about change.

Real change. Not tokens and pacifiers, but something that would endure time.

He didn't want to disappoint Breonna, but at the same time he began to evaluate the options of his position. One thing for sure without a doubt, the fight would definitely continue as long as hateful cops continued to kill unarmed black and brown people.

A caste system of racism has existed for so long in America that now it appeared as if it were the natural order of things. To the point where hate and discrimination was so far deeply embedded that it had become nearly invisible.

These fascist attacks have not only focused on K-12 educational process but have reached way beyond impacting the whole social and political structures and discourse, collectively. Republican legislatures in more than twenty-two states had already proposed anti-critical race theory laws to try to control what can and can't be taught about United States history and racism.

George recognized the looming shadow of a dire situation where systematically black and brown people were being forced to pledge total allegiance to a white Christian fascist America that hated them.

Recently he'd been following the news and reading everything he could get his hands on concerning African history and Critical Race Theory, and he didn't like what he was finding. It was so obvious that white people were overwhelmingly attempting to erase from everyone's memory the truth about slavery and the past it played in making America great.

But what seemed to disturb George the most was the horrors that were unnecessarily committed in order to achieve that greatness that they took so much pride in today. Millions of African men, women and children had to be systematically kidnapped, raped and murdered, lynched, tortured, molested and brutalized in order for whites to reach their goal of greatness.

And for some odd reason white people felt that that part of the history shouldn't and wouldn't be told, no matter what.

Basically that's sort of like telling the Jews to pretend that the Holocaust didn't happen and not to teach their children anything about it. George was deeply in thought pondering these things when Breonna tapped him on the shoulder.

"You first," she said, frowning as the nurse approached them.

George rolled up his sleeve.

After leaving the vaccination site, George took Breonna home and helped her pack her things. About four hours later she had all her stuff sitting in his living room.

"Where am I gonnah put all of this junk?" she said, putting her hands on her hips.

"Wherever you want," he replied. George pulled her to him and gave her a kiss. Breonna melted in his arms. He broke the kiss. She moaned in protest.

"I could have used a little bit more of that," she said crossing her arms over her chest and rolling her eyes at him obviously displeased.

"Don't worry, I'm sure you'll be getting more than your fair share real soon," George said smiling.

"I better," she rolled her eyes again and put her hands back on her wide hips.

"God, she's such a beautiful woman," George thought, as he admired her. He was so lucky to have her. Life had a crazy way of bringing people closer together; that was for sure.

This woman was getting ready to be the mother of his child, which was a wonderful blessing as far as he was a concerned. What more could a man ask for?

Being with her was like heaven on earth. After making love that first time he couldn't recall a moment when he wasn't thinking about her. He felt a little guilty inside for not revealing his true intentions to her. He wanted to tell her the truth, but at the same time he didn't want to disappoint her. He saw the look in her eyes when she told him about the baby. Seeing how happy she was, he couldn't bring himself to take that away from her.

"What you thinking about?" she asked when she saw the concerned look on his face.

"You," he said.

"What about me?"

"Everything."

She smiled, "Everything like what?"

"I wouldn't know where to start."

"I got time."

He paused for a second, "You're an amazing woman Bre."

"Thank you," she said smiling, "And you an amazing man."

He reached for her. She melted into his arms like silk. They embraced. Within a split second their lips were locked together in a lustful, passionate kiss. George sat down on the couch. Breonna climbed on top of him. They found each other's lips again and their tongues began to explore each other's mouths.

Snap, crackle, pop were the sounds their mouths made as they desperately sucked on each other's flesh.

Cupping both of her huge, luscious ass cheeks in both of his hands, George squeezed the soft mounds which seemed to literally melt between his fingers. The throbbing erection inside his pants screamed for attention. It was so hard it hurt. Cleverly he unsnapped her bra, lifted her shirt, and began feasting on a firm breast, giving his undivided attention to a rock-hard nipple.

"Oooh!" Breonna moaned with pleasure when she felt his hot mouth on her sensitive flesh. Her pussy began to throb and beat. She could feel her sticky wetness bubbling between her legs. Finding her other breast, George put his mouth on it and sucked hard on the soft flesh. A single drop of cunt juice ran down the inside of Breonna's thigh as the heat continued to boil between her legs. Her pussy was so wet it began to drip. Slowly she slid off of him onto her knees. She immediately noticed the bulge in his pants and aggressively began tugging on his zipper. George watched her. His heart rate increased when he felt her tiny little hand digging inside his pants. Finally, she found her prize. A sense of joy covered her face. She smiled at him as she continued to yank him free. She seemed to struggle for a moment but clearly she would not be denied. Suddenly it was in her hand, almost twelve inches of luscious black dick. Without a single moment of hesitation she fell on the huge chunk of meat with her mouth, and repeatedly began thrusting it deeply into her throat.

"Aaaaugh! . . . . . . Aaaaugh! . . . . . . Aaaaugh!" George groaned as he watched his dick continuously disappear into her face. Placing both of her hands on his knees to steady herself, Breonna glided up and down the dick with her mouth slowly. She choked on it. She gagged. She made animal-like sounds in the back of her throat, but she never broke her rhythm. George had that feeling again like he was being eaten alive by a monster. And he liked it. He wished for a moment that she would never stop.

Breonna came up off the dick making a loud popping sound with her mouth. She smiled. She began licking the dick like it was her most precious candy bar. She took her time. She wanted to make sure that he enjoyed every moment. She kissed the head of his manliness. She sucked on it. She tenderly ran her teeth across it. A huge tremor ran through George's entire body. Breonna laughed lovingly before taking him into her mouth again and repeatedly plunging him down her throat.

"Uaaaugh!," George groaned when he felt her turn up the heat again. He was mesmerized by her intense love making which only seemed to increase with velocity. Up and down, up and down, back and forth, back and forth she went, as she slowly glided her soft lips over his stiffness. The pleasure was lustfully overwhelming. George didn't know how much more he'd be able to take before he exploded.

Finally he pushed her back. Breonna moaned her frustration. Obviously she wasn't yet finished feasting on the enormous sausage dog she craved so much.

George stood up and began taking off his shirt. As he was pulling the shirt over his head he felt Breonna's mouth return to his pole. He nearly fell back onto the couch when she plunged the dick into her throat several times. He was so overtaken by the intense pleasure, that for a minute it felt like his legs were gone. He placed both of his hands on her shoulders to steady himself. It took every ounce of will power he had to pull away from her again.

"Hey, where you goin?," she said, not pleased at all. "I was just getting started," she whined.

Aggressively George began taking her clothes off. He was rough with her as he jerked and snatched at her clothes. Once he finally got her down to nothing but her bikini panties he didn't waste any time pulling them off of her, he just yanked on the flimsy fabric until they lay in tatters around her feet. Breonna watched him having his way with her. She was silent. She liked what he was doing. Her pussy was so wet it felt like it was raining inside of her.

Suddenly he grabbed her, forcing her on to the couch. He bent her over, hiking her luscious ass into the air.

"Iaaaaaaaaaiah!" she cried when the huge chunk of man meat split her cunt lips apart, and slammed home. The sound of flesh smacking flesh lay heavily in the air as George firmly gripped her hips and pulled her towards his beastly thrusts.

He fucked her hard and slow. He loved the way her ass moved every time he plowed into her. He watched it closely. The picture in his mind was of two giant tear drops about to fall. So soft. So tender. So beautiful. He couldn't help but to admire it. So sweet.

"Iaaaaaaaiiah, you better stooooooooooop," she cried, falling onto her belly. George held her down as he continued to plow inside her. He eased up on her a little bit, but he didn't stop.

Breonna felt like her pussy was being re-modeled as George pointedly turned her cunt walls into jello. Just that quick and she was nearly on her third orgasm already.

"I'm cummin again," she moaned sweetly. George rewarded her by grabbing her around her waist, raising her ass high in the air and fucking the shit out of her.

"Ooooh! . . . Ooooh – Yeess . . . Ooooh – Yeess! . . . fuck me good! . . . fuck me good!" Breonna moaned as George continued to beat the pussy into submission.

Breonna didn't know what the hell was wrong with her. For some reason she couldn't stop cummin this time.

"Oooh God, it's cumin again babe!," she screamed.

"That's what I want! . . . That's it! . . . . Aaaaaaugh! Give that pussy up! Huh! Huh! . . . . Yeah, that's what I'm talking about. Aaaaaugh! Give that pussy up!" George groaned as he continued to beat her back out.

In the middle of her climax George flipped her over onto her back, pushed her little feet back over her head until her toes touched the arm of the couch, then plunged back deeply into her sticky wetness.

"Iaaaaaiah," Breonna cried when she felt the hard piece of stump penetrate her honey dip. George had her legs pinned back so far that when she turned her head to the side her nose touched her ankle. She liked what he did to her. He always seemed to literally fuck her brains out.

Even so, things still seemed a little different this time, because she was cumin non-stop. There's no question that he was definitely hitting the right spots. He was taking here places she'd never been before, and it was somewhere out of this world.

Suddenly George slowed down and started drilling the pussy slowly. He started rotating his hips in that circular motion, and she damn near lost her mind with another orgasm.

"Oooh shit bae! There it is again!" she screamed.

"Oooh God, it won't stop! . . . Oooh God please," she cried as her body began to tremble and shake once again.

George let one of her legs down while keeping the other one firmly pinned back over her head. He dug in the pussy like he was searching for something. Breonna cried out in pleasure. He found what he was looking for, obviously. Breonna was drunk on lust. She was so weak from the multiple orgasms that she'd had, that when George finally let her other leg down it just fell limply to the side. She was now completely in a submissive position with her legs spread widely apart, while George continued to dig for more white gold.

"Ooooh baby please," she cried.

Roughly George turned her over, jacking her ass high into the doggie style position. Breonna tried to brace herself for the long hard massive chunk of meat which immediately split her cunt lips apart and buried itself deeply inside her juicy passage.

Breonna thought she was ready for it, but obviously she must have miscalculated. With the first stroke, George hit the bottom of the pussy. It was a deep stroke. So deep that for a minute Breonna thought that he might have knocked something loose inside of her. Instantly, like magic, she started cumin again. She could feel the wave as it washed over her. Breonna did the best thing she knew how in this situation. Breonna screamed.

"Iaaaaaiiiah! . . . Wait baby! . . . Ooooh! . . . Pleeeease . . . just take it easy, ok," she whined.

George stabbed the pussy hard again. Then again, and again, and again. He beat the pussy up like it was Ike and Tina. What's love got to do wit this.

Breonna was highly impressed with his performance. Welcome home baby momma.

C H A P T E R 3 1

B L U E L I V E S M A T T E R

"Ladies and gentlemen, fellow officers, and all law enforcement agencies of our great country, I want to thank you for coming out today in support of our brave men and women in uniform.

"It's truly a pleasure and an honor to represent those who risk their lives everyday to keep our citizens safe.

"Being fully aware of the uncertainties that you face every day, I want you to know that we deeply understand how difficult this job may be, and we appreciate all the sacrifices that you make to keep America safe.

"Many don't know what it takes to be a cop. Some may think that it's all about putting a badge on your chest and a gun on your waist and that's it, but it's not. There's a whole lot more to it than that. Trust me, I know because I've been there. It takes pride, commitment and dedication. It takes courage. There are a lot of bad people out there, and without law enforcement there would be total chaos. Justice and order would be a thing of the past. That's when I hear all this talk about defunding our police departments. It kind'ah makes me wonder. Personally, I believe that the only people that would want to defund the police are criminals, and their supporters. And I can tell you right now that that's definitely not going to happen, especially not in the state of Texas, where we pride ourselves on being strict enforcers of the law in the country.

"Now on the other hand, you have the Democrats, and a far-left administration that wish to give free reign to these domestic terrorists, who use these social justice organizations as a disguise to organize their supporters and encourage them to commit violent acts against authority figures.

"But surely, as I stand here before you fine citizens, and you brave men and women in uniform today, you may rest assured that this sort of behavior will be highly unacceptable in the lone star state. And together we will face this threat accordingly," said Tarrant County Texas Sheriff, Billy Waybourn.

There was a huge round of applause as officers and their supporters rose to their feet and gave their sheriff's comments a very warm welcome.

Hundreds were in attendance at the blue lives matter rally, which was also being accommodated by a heavy, well-armed police presence. Considering what had happened recently in Minnesota and California, law enforcement agencies all over the country were stepping up their efforts of security and anti-terrorism training. Policing had suddenly become more dangerous than they had ever been since the very formation of America's first police forces. And ongoing efforts were being made in every state to be able to rise to the occasion without pause.

"Folks, currently we have reached a dilemma in this country which is overwhelmingly unavoidable. We must bear witness and accept the fact that society has changed. Our progress as a race has advanced and so has technology. We have collectively increased on many different levels. I need not remind you, but I will, that crime has also advanced. The criminal mind has evolved. And by trying to adapt to this phenomenon we had fallen short of the reality to the actual danger and extent of the internal threat that this country now faces. I think that we can all agree that the main question is, 'what are we going to do about it?' Our forefathers built this great country for us. Are we just supposed to stand by ideally and watch it go to waste?" Sheriff Waybourn said.

"Nooooooh!"

"No way!"

"Hell no!" the crowd jeered as hundreds of supporters and police officers pumped their fists into the air.

Sheriff Waybourn paused for a few seconds, giving the crowd a fair chance to vent some of their anger and frustration before quieting down the crowd by raising his hand for calm.

"I didn't think so," he said. He took a few sips from a glass of water before resuming.

"Now, I know that you all have witnessed the recent and past tragic events in regard to the brutal murders of police. Our hard-working citizens in this country, and many of you are frustrated, and you have a right to be. This is what happens when you get soft on crime. It's like giving the criminals the green light to come after you. I'm sorry, but it's not the way we do things here in Texas. This has been a law-and-order state for more than two-hundred years, and I intend to make sure that it stays that way, personally. With what's going on right now in this country, we can't afford to let our guard down for a second."

There were plenty of chants and nods from the crowd of supporters and police officers as the sheriff continued to make his case. SWAT teams casually patrolled the rally site, fully alert for any possible disturbances. K-9 units patrolled the perimeter. The show of force was astonishing. It might give one the impression of being in some type of military encampment.

Sheriff Waybourn looked out over the crowd of supporters and police personnel. He liked what he saw. A sense of power mixed with pride washed over him. He took another sip of water as he continued to preach his sermon of brimstone and fire in regard to crime, and law and order.

CHAPTER 32

MISSION ACCOMPLISHED

George pulled himself up from under the limp little hand that rested on his chest. Breonna was out cold, lightly snoring like a young baby in a carriage. Mouth slightly ajar with a couple of drops of spit running from the corner of her lips. She was in a fetal position looking like the cutest little thing you've ever seen in your life. George stared at her for a moment. Her beauty was captivating. Her little, tiny feet, so delicate. She meant so much to him. He gently ran his hand through her hair. So soft. So sweet. She was naked. Shaped so perfectly. Juicy. He thought about waking her up by putting her pussy in his mouth, but he decided not to. It was tempting. Just thinking gave him an erection. He promised himself that if she was still asleep when he got back, he was going to wake her up by sticking a nice warm tongue inside her love nest.

He got dressed. It was time to go talk to the rest of the crew and let them know that it was time to chill out for a while. The mission was accomplished. He also wanted to let them know that they needed to get vaccinated. They had already lost one good brother to Covid, and the risk of losing anybody else wasn't worth it. It was time for them to pull out of the drug game and start investing their money in legitimate businesses. Play the perfect citizen. Form something real nice for themselves and their community.

He thought about the sniper rifles that they still had in storage. He had a whole other plan for that. He decided that maybe it would be best to go dough low. One man wrecking team. If a statement needed to be made he'd just get on some James Bond shit and handle it himself. He pondered how could he train himself to be a master assassin. He liked the idea. He even smiled as he thought about it. Then suddenly an overwhelming sense of sadness came over him.

"Why? Why do we have to live like this? It's like the fight against hate and racism is a never-ending battle. Who would even want to live like this? Who wants to be constantly oppressed and reminded over and over of some methodical inferiority and backwardness? Where does this hate come from? Why won't it die?" George thought deeply about these things. He checked his reasoning, "how many people do the police kill every year? Eleven thousand?" He's heard conservatives down-play it, as if eleven thousand people was not a lot because there were over three-hundred million people living in the United States.

Actually, that's eleven thousand times all the family and loved ones that were affected by the tragedy. They always forget to mention that part. But deep down inside he began to realize that Brianna was right, and that maybe it was time to let it go. All that the revenge and hate had ever done was cause death, destruction and pain. He had to walk away from it.

There had to be a better way to bring peace. Brianna inspired him. His heart melted for her. He thought of their unborn child. He was so excited. It was truly a blessed time to be alive.

President Biden was doing everything he could to bring more social justice programs into the fabric of American history and society. But very powerful Republicans in the Senate stood together against his efforts in every way possible to undermine the President's efforts. Finally. An American president had risen who sincerely understood the effects of slavery and how racism and discrimination had destroyed black and brown communities for centuries.

The President was determined to finish the job that Lincoln had started. He was the only President in American history to openly denounce white supremacy and aggressively attempt to assist the needs of poor, black and brown communities. He was truly a build back better president. While Republicans idea of helping the poor were simple tax cuts which mostly favored the rich, the President created programs and businesses that put money into people's pockets.

President Trump was still running around town lying about the election being stolen from him, while the speaker of the house, Nancy remained focused on fortifying the capital and uncovering the January 6th attempted overthrow of the government.

Criminal justice reforms came with sweeping changes to policing and the mass-incarceration of America's citizens.

Big changes were being made in America, even while well-organized white supremacist groups continued to scream America First, the President remained on course to unite the world. The first woman Vice President was a black woman. Who would have ever seen that day coming.

They said Vice President Harris put a lot of men and women in prison when she was Attorney General, and that she was responsible for mass incarceration. But soon as she started designing programs to release prisoners and help them find jobs and earn their rights to vote again, muthahfuckahs started hating.

I guess it comes with the job.

Racism was falling.

It wasn't as powerful as it used to be.

Interracial marriages were at their highest ever in American History.

It's a new day.

All the shit slave masters did to keep white and black people apart had failed.

A new era in time had finally come.

You could feel that something good was going on in America. You could see it on TV. Hear it on the radio.

They demonized the President as a socialist for his bold moves to make reparations for past crimes of slave masters against their former slaves.

He was truly the most outgoing President America had ever seen.

They cried when the job markets didn't grow for months, and inflation was through the roof. But as soon as nearly one million jobs were created, they were kissing the President's ass again.

It was indeed a wonderful time to be alive in America.

Collin Powell died, and everybody paid their respects to a great man.

The Statues of Confederate soldiers and white supremist rulers were continuing to be torn down. The strive to be a just society in America was strengthening.

An unstoppable force was in motion.

The Black Lives Matter movement grew into a worldwide movement.

The world was finally changing.

After informing the crew about the change in plans, it seemed like everybody was more in agreement than what he'd actually realized.

"They say that everything happens for a reason in its season."

Finally, he made it back home. He entered the house. Everything was quiet. It was dark. He took off his shoes and walked up the stairs barefoot.

By the time he reached the top of the steps he was naked.

The bedroom door was slightly ajar. He pushed it open with his toe.

On the bed directly in front of him Breonna laid on her side, still sleeping like a baby.

George climbed onto the bed. He admired her beauty for a few moments before rolling her over onto her back. And within that same motion, he planted his lips against the soft folds of her juicy cunt and began to suck on the silky flesh hungrily.

"Muuuummmmmmmmnn!" Breonna moaned as she realized that she'd just been awakened by a hot delicious tongue probing inside of her pussy. He'd startled her.

She moaned her approval of the rude awakening as she wrapped her legs around George's neck and cupped his head between her legs tighter. She whimpered as the hot, wet mouth continued to devour her sticky, slick folds. It felt like she was being turned into a puddle of water. She melted.

Being woken up by a long hot tongue slithering inside of her pussy was out of this world.

She couldn't even talk. All she could do was grunt and make animal-like sounds.

She was getting ready to cum on that probing tongue. That little hot member that was digging around inside of her love tunnel.

Suddenly Breonna tensed. She squeezed her legs even tighter around George's neck while holding his head firmly between her legs. She cried out.

She began to twitch and buck against that wanting mouth, and that invading little hot tongue. She began to cum. Hard.

She melted all over again.

It was a wonderful time to be alive in America.

The end? Maybe not.

Black Vigilantes.

THAH XAH QSHUNAH